# LAW OF THE NOOSE

*by*

Alan Irwin

**Dales Large Print Books**
Long Preston, North Yorkshire,
BD23 4ND, England.

British Library Cataloguing in Publication Data.

Irwin, Alan
    Law of the noose.

    A catalogue record of this book is
    available from the British Library

    ISBN   978-1-84262-549-1 pbk

First published in Great Britain in 1996 by Robert Hale Limited

Published in Large Print 2007 by arrangement with
Robert Hale Limited

Dales Large Print is an imprint of Library Magna Books Ltd.

Printed and bound in Great Britain by
T.J. (International) Ltd., Cornwall, PL28 8RW

# LAW OF THE NOOSE

# ONE

Joe Kilgour finished saddling his horse, and paused for a moment before leading it over to the ranch-house, where his wife Alice was standing on the doorstep, waiting to bid him goodbye. Joe was a tall, lean man, in his fifties, grey-haired and bearded, and neatly dressed. His wife Alice, younger than her husband by several years, was a small, sprightly, cheerful-looking woman.

Slowly, Joe's gaze passed over the neat two-storey timber-built ranch-house, then the bunkhouse, barn and corral, all structures on which he had toiled long and hard, before pronouncing himself satisfied. His gaze lifting, he looked across the pasture and the river, and over his range to the distant Rocky Mountains. It was a view of which he never tired.

Travelling north from Texas, and trailing a small herd with him, he had arrived in Southern Colorado three years earlier, with his wife, and his son Jack. He bought a stretch of land along the Arkansas River, established a small ranch, the Diamond K, and prospered. After two years, Joe hired two hands, Jim Morgan and Cliff Evans, and shortly afterwards Jack rode off to help an old friend of his, Burt Lawrence, who had married, and started ranching, in a small way, near Fort Worth, Texas. Burt's wife, Ellen, had sent word to Jack that Burt had been shot by rustlers, and badly needed help. Jack's parents had heard nothing from him until a month ago, when a message arrived, saying he would be coming home shortly.

Having recently bought a further stretch of land along the river, Joe was anxious to have more cattle on the spread as soon as possible, and a few days previously, he had spoken with a drover who had driven several herds along the Goodnight-Loving Trail from Texas to Denver, Colorado. This trail had been established by cattlemen Charles Goodnight and Oliver Loving, in 1866, for driving cattle from ranches in Texas to Colorado, via New Mexico Territory. The trail avoided Comanche country in North Texas.

The drover had told him that the Lazy B Ranch in the Texas Panhandle regularly sent batches of breeding cattle north into Colorado. He said that Todd Burley, the owner of the Lazy B, who specialized in breeding and calf production, would probably include any cattle that Joe might want, on the next drive north. On hearing this, Joe decided to ride to the Lazy B, to see if he could strike a deal with Burley.

He walked his horse over to his wife.

'Should be back in nine or ten days,' he said. 'Maybe Jack'll turn up before I get back. You'll be all right?'

'I'll be all right, Joe,' she replied, 'with Cliff and Jim around. You know I don't like it when you're away, but I guess you've got to go.'

Joe mounted his horse. It was a handsome animal – a big gelding, completely white, except for a black patch on its tail. On his head, Joe wore a new, broad-brimmed Texas hat, also completely white, except for a Texas star on one side of the crown. Joe was a man who took pride in his appearance.

'We sure need more cattle,' he said, turning his horse to face south. He rode past the barn, heading for the open range. A quarter of a mile further on, he turned in the saddle, looked back towards Alice, waved, then continued on his way.

Heading almost due south, roughly parallel

9

to the Goodnight-Loving Cattle Trail, Joe crossed the border into New Mexico Territory two days later, then headed south-east for the Texas Panhandle, and the Lazy B. Around noon the following day, he approached four homesteads, along the bank of a narrow river. As he was passing the first one, he saw a man working in a field close to the track. He stopped, and asked the man the direction of the nearest town.

'That's Drago,' said the man. 'Five miles east of here.'

After a brief conversation with the homesteader, Joe thanked him, and rode on to Drago. He bought a few provisions at the store, then headed for the Texas border, which he crossed late in the day, and camped there for the night. He figured he should reach the Lazy B in two days' time.

The following morning, he passed into an area where cows were grazing. He rode close to a bunch of them, to take a look at the brand. It was 'JW', the brand of a rancher Jason Weaver, who ran a big spread in the Panhandle. Joe had heard of him, from time to time. He headed for a low flat-topped hill which lay in his path, then swung right to pass round its base. He was halfway round, when a party of four Comanche braves, on horseback, and all carrying rifles, appeared in view from behind the hill, whooping loudly, and headed straight for him, at full speed.

Joe wheeled his mount, and urged it into a gallop. He aimed for a group of small hills in a rugged stretch of broken ground visible in front of him. Maybe, he thought, if he rode fast, he could find some cover there from which to defend himself.

He had a good mount, and glancing backwards after the chase had continued for about half a mile, he could see that he had gained a little ground. When he reached the broken ground, he headed for a distant narrow valley, visible between two ridges. He looked backwards again, and saw that he was still further ahead of his pursuers.

As he drew close to the entrance to the valley, he heard the sound of rifle fire coming from ahead and above. He glanced upwards, and could see riflemen firing from the slopes bordering the valley. They were directing their fire at the approaching Comanches. Joe rode into the valley, dismounted behind a large boulder, pulled his rifle from the saddle holster, and added his fire to that already being directed at the Indians. He could see that two of them were already down. He dropped one himself, then saw the remaining brave fall.

He turned, and looked up the valley. There was a small herd grazing several hundred yards away. Then he looked up the slopes, and saw four men, two on each slope, walking towards him. All four men had their rifles pointing in his general direction. He replaced his rifle in the saddle holster, then stood still, watching the approaching men. They joined up on the floor of the valley, and walked towards him. His first thought had been that the men were JW ranch-hands, but as they drew closer, he knew he had been mistaken. They were a hardbitten quartet, all bearded, and they looked as if they'd been sleeping rough for some time. Each of them wore a single gun, on his right hip.

The four men stopped in front of Joe, and eyed him for a few moments. Then one of them spoke. He was a tall, thin man, about the same build as Joe himself. His name was Duggan. His eyes, holding Joe's, were hard.

'You had a bit of luck there, mister,' he observed. 'Hadn't been for us, you'd likely have had your scalp lifted by now. Who are you, and what are you doing in these parts?'

Glancing up the valley, Joe could see a

small campfire between him and the small herd, and four horses tied to a picket line. As he turned his head back, to answer the tall man, he had a growing suspicion that he and his pursuers had interrupted the operations of a gang of rustlers. However, he could see no reason to lie to them. If he could convince them that he was a stranger in these parts, maybe they would let him ride on.

'Name's Kilgour,' he said. 'Riding from Colorado down to the Lazy B, south of here. I figure to buy some cattle there.'

Duggan spoke to the man on his right, a strongly-built man, around medium height, with a swarthy complexion, and a pock-marked face. On the side of his face, in the form of a V, were a couple of long scars. Probably caused during a fight, by a couple of knife slashes, thought Joe. The man's name was Barrett, Clem Barrett.

'Search him, Clem,' said Duggan. 'Then have a look in his saddlebags. And you Frank,' he said to one of the others, 'climb up to that rock there, and keep a lookout.'

He pointed to a rock, partially embedded in the ground, near the top of the slope leading out of the valley.

Frank walked away, and Duggan held his

rifle on Joe, as Barrett checked the rancher's pockets. He found nothing there. Then he walked over to Joe's horse, and looked in the saddlebags. He walked back to Duggan with some banknotes, and a sheet of paper in his hand, and handed them over.

Duggan told Barrett to take Joe's horse to the picket line, then he checked the banknotes, and stuffed them in his pocket. After that, he took a look at the paper. It was a letter from the president of the bank in Pueblo, Colorado, through which Joe conducted his business affairs. Joe had brought it along, as proof of his bona fides, to show to Burley of the Lazy B.

'Looks like you're telling the truth, mister,' said Duggan, folding the paper, and putting it in his own pocket. 'Question is, what are we going to do with you? You ain't exactly welcome here.'

Suddenly, the lookout called urgently from above.

'Riders coming this way,' he shouted, pointing to the south-east. 'Six or seven, I reckon.'

'Watch this man,' said Duggan to Barrett, then turned and ran up to the lookout's position. Looking towards the south-east, he saw the approaching riders. They were still some distance away, riding at a canter.

14

Accompanied by the lookout, he ran back down the slope to Barrett.

'JW riders, for sure,' he said. 'I reckon we'd better head for those other cattle Mort's holding east of here, and when we get there, we'd better start driving them east, before things get too hot for us here. We'll have more than enough time to meet up with Travis in The Indian Territory, and hand the cattle over.

'We've got to get out of here before they see us,' he went on. 'If we ride up the valley fast, we should be well out of sight before they find the cattle. And all to the good if we can get them to hang around for a while when they get here. And I've got an idea how we can do that, so's we can make a clean getaway.'

He walked around Joe, as if heading towards the fire. Then, suddenly, he turned, pulling his gun, and stepped up behind Joe. Quickly, he raised the barrel of the gun, and fired it close to Joe's head, so that the bullet gouged a furrow along the side of the rancher's head, above the ear. Joe fell to the ground, unconscious.

Duggan picked up Joe's smart Texas hat, and threw his own battered headgear on the ground. Then he went for Joe's horse, and

15

mounted it. He rode back to Joe, and dropped the rancher's rifle on the ground near him, and Barrett replaced the gun which he had taken from Joe's holster. Barrett, on the way to his horse, bent down to pick up a running iron which was lying near the fire, but Duggan told him to leave it be. He ordered his men to make it look as though only one man had been with the cattle when the Indians attacked. Then, leaving Duggan's horse behind, the four men rode fast up the valley, and were out of sight well before the approaching riders reached the dead Indians outside the entrance to the valley.

When Joe came to, it was a while before he collected his senses. His ears were ringing, his head was throbbing, and he was having difficulty in focusing his eyes. He was dimly aware of a pain in his side, as if something was striking him intermittently. He shook his head, sat up, and suddenly his eyes snapped into focus, and he saw seven men standing in front of him. The man closest to him was just about to deliver another kick into his side. As the man's foot moved forward, Joe rolled to one side, and avoided the worst of the blow. Then he sat up again, and holding his head, he looked up at the

16

men standing in front of him.

Jason Weaver, owner of the JW, was at the centre of the group. He was holding the running iron in his hand. He was a short, stocky man, with massive shoulders, and a hard, ruthless face. It was rumoured that his rise from cowboy to his present status as owner of a ranch which was large by any standards, had not been unaccompanied by a certain amount of land-grabbing, and intimidation of homesteaders and small stockmen. He spoke to the man beside him, his foreman Walt Stringer, a tall, lean, saturnine man, with a drooping moustache.

'Looks like we've caught this man red-handed, Walt,' he said. 'He sure knows how to use a rifle, finishing off four Comanches like that. He must have been hit on the head just as he killed the last one.'

He spoke to Joe.

'You got anything to say, mister, before we hang you from one of those trees over there?' he asked, pointing to three cotton-woods standing a little way along the floor of the valley, close to the river.

Fighting back a rising panic, Joe forced himself to speak quietly.

'You're making a mistake,' he said, 'I'm no rustler. My name is Kilgour. I own the

17

Diamond K Ranch in Colorado, east of Pueblo. I was heading for the Lazy B Ranch, to buy some cattle, when those four Comanches out there started chasing me. There were four men in the valley here. They started shooting at the Comanches, and downed three of them. I got the fourth. Then they got the drop on me, but when they spotted you coming, they lit out fast. But before they did that, they fired a bullet along the side of my head here, that knocked me out for a while.' He moved his hand away from his head, to reveal the deep bullet-graze.

'You got some gall, expecting us to believe a tall story like that,' said Weaver. 'I was talking with Burley only two days ago, and he didn't say nothing about a buyer from Colorado coming to see him. You got any proof that says you ain't a thieving rustler?'

'Burley didn't know I was coming,' said Joe, 'but you can check my horse. It has the Diamond K brand on it.'

He pointed towards the picket line, then stared in shocked disbelief as he saw the horse which was standing there. It was not his.

'They've taken my horse,' he said, knowing that he now had with him no shred of evidence to prove his real identity.

'That so?' said Weaver. 'You must think we're fools, to believe a story like the one you've just told us. If those four men you talked about got the drop on you, how come you're wearing a six-gun, and how come your rifle's still here?'

Almost in despair, Joe looked down at the loaded gun in his holster.

'I don't know,' he said.

Weaver turned to his foreman.

'Take his gun, Walt,' he said, 'then have a look at the sign, and tell me how many rustlers you reckon have been in this valley, apart from this one here.' He pointed to Joe.

Stringer slowly walked to the fire, then around it, studying the ground. Then he walked over to the picket line, and up the valley for a short distance, continuing to look closely at the ground. Then he came back to Weaver.

'You know I don't claim to be a real expert at tracking, boss,' he said, 'but I figure there were another four men here, because I could just make out the tracks of four horses heading up the valley. Just how old those tracks are, I don't know. The ground's too hard for me to tell. Maybe one or two days, maybe less. I just ain't a good enough tracker to say.'

'They must have ridden off to collect some more cattle,' said Weaver. 'And this one stayed behind to keep an eye on the herd. I reckon we should watch out for them coming back here. Might save a lot of time that way. Meantime, we can tend to this one.'

He spoke to Joe.

'We ain't been bothered by rustlers till you and your friends came along,' he said, 'but I've always figured the best way to deal with rustlers, if they ever did turn up, would be to string them up pronto, before the law could interfere.'

'I've told you who I am,' said Joe struggling to keep his voice calm. 'I know I ain't carrying any proof of it, because the rustlers took all my belongings. But all you have to do is to postpone this hanging for a while, and send a telegraph message to Sheriff Colby in Pueblo. He knows me well. And he knows I was heading for the Lazy B. I told him so.'

'It's clear,' said Weaver, to his foreman, 'that this man's just playing for time. Maybe he thinks his friends'll come along and rescue him.'

One of Weaver's men, who he had sent to have a look at the herd, came back to report

20

to him.

'They're all JW cattle,' he said.

Weaver looked at the running iron he was still holding in his hand.

'That settles it,' he said.

He turned, and pointed to two of his men in turn. 'You men,' he ordered. 'Drive these cattle to the west range. Then go back to the ranch-house.'

He waited until the men had driven the cattle out of the valley. Then, glaring at Joe, he spoke to two of his men, Sully and Quaid.

'Hold his arms, and take him down to those trees,' he ordered, then, turning to Stringer, he told him to follow along with a horse and some rope.

Joe resisted at first, but the men holding him were both strong men, and after they had dragged him a few yards, he walked along, between them. When they reached the first of the three cottonwoods, Weaver, who was following behind, stopped them. Desperately, Joe spoke to him again.

'You're making a big mistake,' he said. 'I've told you who I am, and you can easily check up on it. If you hang me now, you're just plain murderers.'

He looked around the group of men

surrounding him. It consisted of Weaver, his foreman Stringer, and three JW hands, Randle, Sully and Quaid. Only one of the men, Randle, looked ill at ease, and averted his gaze as Joe's eyes met his. The others stared right back at him, hostility in their eyes.

'I'm tired of hearing this rustler talk,' said Weaver. 'Put a gag on him, Quaid. And tie his hands behind him.'

When this had been done, a rope with a noose was thrown over a high branch, and a horse, with saddle removed, was brought up under the noose, and held there. Then Joe was forcibly hoisted up by Sully and Stringer, to sit on the horse. The noose was placed around his neck, and the free end of the rope was fastened around the tree trunk, so that the rope was taut. Weaver stood beside the horse, with a quirt in his hand.

'You behind me in this?' he asked the four men who were standing watching him. They all nodded, except Randle, who hesitated, then spoke.

'This ain't right, Mr. Weaver,' he said. 'We should check his story before we lynch him.'

Weaver ignored him, and shouted to Quaid and Sully, who were holding the horse, to let go. As they did so, Weaver quirted it hard, across the haunch. The horse leapt forward, and Joe's body fell downward, then jerked to a stop, with his feet just clear of the ground. The body swung and rotated for a while, with a slight jerking of the legs, until finally it came to rest, except for a slight swinging motion set up by the breeze.

Weaver spoke to the four men with him.

'Nobody gets to know about this,' he warned, 'or we'll all be in trouble with the law. We'll cut him down, and bury him. And remember, anybody opens their mouth about this, he's got me to answer to.

'Tomorrow morning, Walt,' he went on, 'send two men out here, to wait for those rustlers coming back. And tell them if they see any sign of them, to ride in fast, and let us know.'

# TWO

Jack Kilgour arrived at the Diamond K Ranch on the same day that his father died by hanging, out on the JW range. His mother, who had seen him riding up, greeted him outside the ranch-house, and told him of his father's visit to the Lazy B Ranch in the Texas Panhandle.

Jack was in his late twenties, about as tall as his father, but broader in the shoulder. He was clean-shaven, and had his mother's blue eyes and cheerful expression. He was dressed in cowboy clothes of good quality.

'As near as I can figure,' his mother told him, 'your father will be back here in five or six days. You aiming to stay here for a spell?'

'I haven't decided yet,' replied Jack, 'but I'll hang on here to lend a hand till father gets back.'

'What happened at Burt and Ellen's place?' she asked.

'All settled down there nice and quiet,' Jack replied. 'Burt's fine again now, and with a bit of help from the law, we got rid of the rustlers.'

Jack's mother looked at him thoughtfully, and glanced at the Colt Peacemaker lying snugly, in its tied-down holster, against Jack's right hip. She knew that Jack had a natural aptitude for handling guns, and that he was a crack shot both with revolver and rifle. It worried her sometimes, that maybe his talents in that direction might lead him into trouble. Joe scoffed at her concerns.

'A man's got to be able to look after himself nowadays,' he said. 'And we both know Jack well enough to be sure he'd never turn bad. It just ain't in his nature.'

Five days later, Alice started watching out for her husband, but on that day, and during the following six days, there was no sign of him. She expressed her worry to Jack at supper time.

'I can't understand it', she said. 'He said he'd only stay at the Lazy B maybe a couple of days, then he'd head back home. He's near a week overdue. He'd have let me know, if he knew he was going to be late back.'

'Give it another day,' said Jack, ' and if he isn't back by then, I'll telegraph a message to the Lazy B.'

This he did, two days later, when his

father had still not shown up. In his message, he asked Burley of the Lazy B whether his father had turned up there, and if he had, when he had left for home.

Jack picked the reply up in Pueblo two days later, in the morning. It read: 'No knowledge Joe Kilgour Diamond K. He has not been here. Burley.'

Jack took the message back to the ranch, and showed it to his mother. The worry in her eyes was evident.

'What can we do, Jack?' she asked.

'I'm leaving today,' he replied. 'I'll follow father's trail as close as I can, and I'll head for the Lazy B, in case he turned up there after Burley sent us that message. And as soon as I get any news, I'll telegraph you.'

'Do that right away, Jack,' she said. 'As soon as you've got any news at all. It's going to be mighty hard, just sitting here, waiting to hear from you.'

'I'll let you know how things are going, mother,' promised Jack. 'I expect father was riding the white gelding, wasn't he?'

She nodded.

'And he was wearing that white Texas hat of his,' she said.

Jack left an hour later, following the route he expected his father would have taken.

Three days later, in New Mexico Territory, heading for the Texas border, Jack rode into Drago. He figured there was a good chance that his father had called there. He went into the general store, and describing his father, he asked the storekeeper if he had seen him recently.

'Sure,' replied the storekeeper. 'He called in two or three weeks ago. Bought a few supplies. Said he was heading for the Panhandle.'

'Seemed all right, did he?' asked Jack.

'Looked well enough to me,' replied the storekeeper. 'Pretty spry, I thought, and smart, too, riding that big white horse, and wearing that white Texas hat.'

Jack thanked the storekeeper, then continued his ride towards the border. He crossed it at sundown, and camped there for the night. The following morning, he decided he would head straight for the Lazy B, in case his father had turned up there after Burley had sent his telegram.

He could see by the cattle he was passing, that he was crossing JW range. Then, late in the day, he crossed a long, low ridge, and camped for the night on the far side. Soon after he set off the following morning, he saw some Lazy B cattle, growing larger in number as he progressed.

Around mid-afternoon, Jack heard voices as he was passing through a narrow gap between two low, flat-topped hills. On the other side of the gap, the track veered to the right, and about twenty yards along it, Jack could see a girl, apparently in a heated conversation with two men. The two men were standing near their horses, and one of them was holding the bridle of the horse on which the girl was seated.

The girl was slim and good-looking, with auburn hair falling to her shoulders. She was wearing a riding-skirt, and a large wide-brimmed hat. The two men were roughly dressed, in cowhands' clothing. Both were slightly below average height. One was slim and clean-shaven, with sandy hair, the other was broader, and bearded. Both men were wearing right-hand guns.

The three caught sight of Jack as he emerged from the gap, and turned to ride towards them. One of the men spoke sharply to the girl, making a gesture towards Jack, who was out of earshot. The hands of the two men moved to rest on the handles of their six-guns. Jack rode up to the trio, and stopped about twelve feet away, facing them.

The bearded man scowled up at Jack.

'You can ride straight on, stranger,' he said. 'This is just a talk we're having with the boss's daughter here. It's no concern of yours.'

Jack could tell by the look on the girl's face, that she was very apprehensive about something. He was just about to speak to her, when the bearded man spoke again, more forcibly this time.

'I told you to ride on, stranger,' he said. 'You going now, or d'you want us to help you on your way?'

Watching the two men closely, Jack got down from his horse, and stood facing them. He glanced up at the girl, whose horse was still being held by the sandy-haired man. He could see the fear in her eyes.

'You all right, miss?' he asked.

She hesitated for a moment, looking first at the two men, then back at Jack. Then suddenly, she made up her mind.

'No!' she shouted. 'These men are trying to kidnap me.'

As she spoke, she pulled hard on the reins of her horse, which moved backwards.

The bearded man went for his gun. He made a fast draw, but it looked clumsy against the swift, smooth precision with which Jack's Peacemaker was lifted from its holster, was cocked, and was fired at the bearded man's chest. The sandy-haired man, still holding on to the bridle of the girl's horse with his left hand, also drew his gun, but his draw was slower than his partner's, and as the girl's horse moved backwards, then reared at Jack's shot, his aim was disturbed. His shot, aimed at Jack, went wide by a few inches, and Jack's second shot dropped him, to lay on the ground close to his partner.

The girl's horse, startled by the shooting, ran off for a short distance, but she soon had it under control. She rode back to Jack, who, seeing that she was all right, had turned to look down at the two men. Both had been shot in the chest, over the heart. White-faced, she stared down at the two bodies on the ground.

'Are they dead?' she asked.

'Yes,' replied Jack. 'Both of them. Did you know them?'

'Yes,' she replied. 'The bearded one was called Parker, the other one Willis. They were hands on the Lazy B, that's my father's ranch.'

'Your father's Mr. Burley?' asked Jack.

'Yes,' she replied. 'His foreman sacked

these two men a couple of days ago, because he reckoned they weren't pulling their weight. They didn't seem to know a lot about looking after cattle. And they were a surly pair. Didn't get on with the other hands. So after they'd been here a couple of weeks, he paid them off.'

She paused, and looked down at the two men again. Jack looked at her face. Despite the shock of seeing two men die in front of her, she already seemed to have herself well under control. A gutsy lady, thought Jack. She looked up, and spoke to him again.

'Parker told me,' she said, 'that they were taking me to a hideout west of here, where I'd have to stay until my father paid a ransom for me. He told me that somebody in South Texas had told them my father was a rich man with a daughter, so they'd ridden up this way with some friends of theirs, with a kidnap in mind. It seemed to them it might be an easy way of making some money.

'When they saw you coming,' she went on, 'they told me to keep my mouth shut, or else they'd kill both you and me. But you looked to me like you might be handy with a gun, and I figured if I slowed Willis down, maybe you could handle them both.'

'You did right,' said Jack. 'If those two men

had taken you, maybe you'd never have seen the Lazy B again.'

'That's how I figured it,' she said. 'What do we do now?'

'So happens I was on my way to see your father,' replied Jack, 'so I'll go along with you. My name's Kilgour, Jack Kilgour. We'd better take these two along with us.'

He went for the two mens' horses, which were grazing nearby, and lifted the two bodies across their backs. He roped the horses together, then mounted and rode off, with the girl by his side. The horses carrying the bodies followed on behind them.

Todd Burley, owner of the Lazy B, a tall, lean man in his fifties, was walking from the barn back to the ranch-house, with his foreman, Ned Jasper, a tough-looking, weather-beaten ex-cowhand, who had been with him for many years. A distant movement out on the range caught Burley's attention. He stopped in his stride, and with Jasper by his side, he looked intently towards it for a while. He could see four horses. One of them, he was sure, was his daughter Mary's, with her in the saddle. Two of the others were carrying something across their backs, and the fourth was carrying another rider.

Burley and Jasper ran to a couple of saddled horses standing outside the bunk-house, mounted, and headed fast for the approaching riders. When they reached them, Jack and the girl came to a halt. Burley stared at the two bodies on the horses' backs, dismounted and looked at the faces of the two dead men, and their wounds. Then he looked up at his daughter.

'You all right, Mary?' he asked.

'I'm all right,' she replied, 'thanks to Mr Kilgour here.'

She went on to tell her father how Parker and Willis had stopped her, and told her what they intended to do, and how Jack had intervened.

'I'm sure glad you happened to be riding by, Mr. Kilgour,' said Burley. 'Things have come to a pretty pass when my daughter ain't safe riding across Lazy B range.'

He mounted his horse, and led the way towards the ranch-house. As they approached it, he told Jasper to get a hand to take the two bodies to the sheriff in Boredo, a town about five miles distant, and to tell him what had happened. Burley and his daughter dismounted. Burley looked up at Jack.

'I'd be obliged if you'd come inside,' he

said. 'I'd like a few words with you. We'll just wait till Ned has sent that hand on his way.'

Jasper joined them shortly, and all four went into the house, and sat down in the living-room.

'Those two men,' said Burley. 'We only took them on because we had a lot of work to get through, and there was a shortage of good hands at the time. But we could see right away they weren't any good as cowhands. Looks like they just wanted to sign on so as to pick up any information that might help them work out a plan to kidnap Mary. It was mighty lucky for us that you happened to be riding across Lazy B range today.'

'So happens,' said Jack, 'I was on my way to see you. I telegraphed you not long ago, from the Diamond K Ranch in Colorado, about my father, Joe Kilgour. I got your answer. Thanks for sending it. Did my father turn up after you sent that telegram off?'

Burley shook his head. 'No, he didn't,' he replied. 'You reckon he's gone missing?'

'It looks like it,' replied Jack. 'He was figuring to ride straight down here to talk to you about buying some Lazy B breeding cattle, then he was going to ride straight home. I know he got as far as Drago, New

Mexico Territory. He called in the general store there. Looks like something happened to him somewhere between Drago and the Lazy B. You ain't heard of any trouble anywhere that might account for him being missing?'

'We've had a few Comanches around, raising hell,' replied Burley, 'but I ain't heard of any white man being killed.

'I'm sorry about your father,' he went on. 'Is your mother back at the Diamond K?'

'She is,' replied Jack. 'And near worried out of her mind.'

'I can guess,' said Burley. 'What d'you plan to do now?'

'I'm going to ride back the way I came,' replied Jack, 'but a lot slower this time. I have a good idea of the route my father would have taken. I'm going to have a good look along that route, and on either side of it, to see if I can see any sign of him or his horse.'

Burley looked at the darkening sky outside.

'Nothing you can do today,' he said. 'You're welcome to stay the night. And come morning, Ned'll send a few hands with you, to help you search over the Lazy B range. You know that the JW Ranch is on the other side of our north boundary, so, coming from Drago, your father would be bound to ride over JW range for a spell.

'Jason Weaver owns that ranch,' Burley went on. 'I meet up with him now and again. He sure knows cattle, but he's not a man you can warm to. Pretty ruthless, I'd say.'

Not long after, they took supper, then sat down in the living-room again, talking. There was a knock on the door. Mary went to open it. The ranch-hand who had taken the bodies of Willis and Parker into Boredo, was standing outside. Mary took a sheet of paper from him, and brought it to her father.

'Telegram, father,' she said.

Burley read the telegram before he realized it wasn't intended for him. His eyes widened as he read it. He handed it to Jack.

'It's for you,' he said.

Jack looked over the message twice, before the full import sank in. It read: 'Your mother very ill. Heart trouble. Get back quick as you can. Jim.'

'I have to leave,' said Jack. 'Right now. I'll camp out on the trail later on.'

He handed the telegram to Mary and Jasper to read. Jasper handed it back to him.

'Get some provisions together, Mary,' said Burley.

Jack left twenty minutes later. As Mary handed the provisions over, he thanked her.

'We hope you find your mother all right,' she said. 'And I hope we'll see you back here one day.'

'That goes for me too,' said Burley. 'Now, before you go, tell us what your father looks like, and tomorrow, Ned will have hands out scouring the range between here and the JW boundary. If we find any trace of your father, I'll let you know right away. And I'll get word to Weaver to watch out for your father, as well.'

# THREE

Jack got back to the Diamond K as fast as he could, with the minimum amount of rest for his horse and himself. As he rode up to the ranch-house, he could see Doc Randall's buggy outside, and as he dismounted, the doctor came out of the house with Jim Morgan. Jack walked over to Randall.

'How is she, doc?' he asked.

Randall shook his head.

'I'm afraid, Jack,' he said, 'you've arrived just too late. Your mother died ten minutes ago.'

Badly shocked, Jack was silent for a few moments. Then he spoke to the doctor again.

'How did it happen, doc?' he asked. 'You know mother was pretty well, generally, though she got a bit tired at times.'

'It was her heart, Jack,' replied the doctor. 'It just decided it didn't want to work any more. I kept it going for a while, but in the end, there was nothing I could do about it. And the worry about your father didn't make things any better. Without that, I reckon she might just have pulled through. But even then, she'd have had to take things pretty easy for the rest of her life.

'Any news of your father?' he went on.

'He was seen passing through Drago, New Mexico Territory,' replied Jack, 'but he never arrived at the Lazy B. I was just going to start out on a search for him, when I got the news about mother.'

'You'll bury your mother here, Jack?' the doctor asked, as he prepared to leave.

'Yes,' replied Jack. 'On the slope of that hill over there, where she liked to sit sometimes. I'd be obliged if you'd ask the undertaker to come out here.'

'I'll do that,' promised the doctor.

On the day of the funeral, after the ceremony was over, and the mourners had departed, Jack had a talk with Jim Morgan. Jim had worked on the Diamond K for the past three years, and he was more a friend than just an ordinary cowhand. He knew everything there was to know about running a small ranch.

'Jim,' said Jack. 'I've got to ride back to the Panhandle to try and find out what's happened to my father. I don't know how long I'll be gone. I'd like you to take charge here while I'm away. I can't think of anybody who would do the job better. And there'd be extra pay, of course. And you'd have to hire another hand. You'd need him, to keep up with the work. Will you do it?'

'Sure I will,' replied Jim. 'You get off soon as you can. Don't worry about things here. I'm hoping the next time you ride in, your father'll be with you.'

Jack left the following morning, and headed for the Lazy B. He knew that Burley would have let him know if any trace of his father had been found, but he felt he should have another talk with the rancher, before he resumed his search in earnest. Burley knew the country in the area, and he knew the people. Maybe he would have some ideas that would help Jack in his search.

And then there was Mary. Despite the distractions, he had thought of her a lot since he had last seen her and her father. He had admired her courage during the encounter with Parker and Willis, and he welcomed the chance of seeing her again.

He saw nothing of interest on the way to the Lazy B. Both Burley and his daughter were in the ranch-house when he arrived there, in the late afternoon. Mary invited him inside. Jack told them of his mother's death, and of his resolve to find out what had happened to his father. They offered their condolences.

'I know how you feel,' said Mary. 'I lost my own mother two years ago. Father and I are still grieving.'

'We found no trace of your father on the Lazy B,' Burley told Jack. 'We had three men searching the north range for a couple of days, but they came up with nothing. And I sent word to Weaver of the JW that your father was missing. Weaver sent word back that he hadn't been seen on the JW.'

'I think I'll ride up to see Weaver,' said Jack. 'We know my father had to cross JW range to get here. I'm going to search that area thoroughly, but I'd better see Weaver first. I reckon.'

'You're welcome to stay the night here,' said Burley.

'Thanks,' said Jack. 'I'll leave in the morning, then. And I sure do appreciate you sending your men out to search for my father.'

He left early, taking leave of Burley, who was still at breakfast. Mary walked outside with him, and waited while he saddled his horse.

'I hope you soon find out what happened

to your father,' she said. 'You must be very worried.'

'I sure am,' said Jack. 'He'd never disappear like that if he had any say in the matter. So he's either had an accident, or he's been killed or wounded, or for some reason he's been taken away by force. One way or another, I've got to find out just what's happened to him.'

'You'll come back, and let us know?' she asked.

'I'll be sure to do that,' replied Jack, 'and, once again, many thanks for your help so far.'

He headed north, and the girl stood looking after him for a while, then went indoors to her father.

'Father,' she said, 'd'you think Jason Weaver could have anything to do with the fact that Mr Kilgour is missing?'

'Weaver is an unscrupulous man,' replied Burley. 'I never liked him. But I can't see any possible reason why a complete stranger like Kilgour, riding across his range, and doing him no harm, should have fallen foul of him.'

When Jack had crossed the north boundary of the Lazy B, he headed for the JW ranch buildings, following directions given to him by Burley. He camped out overnight, and reached his destination during the afternoon of the following day.

A short, stocky man came out of the house as he approached, and stood watching him. Jack rode towards the man, and stopped in front of him.

'My name's Kilgour,' said Jack. 'Would you be Mr. Weaver?'

'The same,' said Weaver. 'I guess you're the one Burley told me about. Come inside.'

Jack dismounted, tied his horse to the hitching-rail, and followed Weaver into the house. He sat down with the rancher in the living-room.

'Seeing as you're here,' said Weaver, 'I guess your father's still missing?'

'He is,' said Jack. 'Last seen in Drago, then vanished without trace, up to now.'

'Well,' said Weaver, 'like I told Burley, we ain't seen no sign of your father on the JW. Burley gave us his description, and I passed it on to all my men. Was he a fit man?'

'None fitter,' replied Jack.

Weaver was just about to speak again, when a young girl ran down the stairs, across to the rancher, and sat on the couch by his side. She was a pretty child, probably around twelve, thought Jack, with dark eyes

43

and hair. Weaver put his arm around her, and she smiled up at him. The rancher smiled back at her.

'This is my daughter Emily,' he told Jack.

'Hello, Emily,' said Jack. She gave him a shy smile.

'My men have covered a lot of range just lately,' continued Weaver, 'including the route your father would probably have taken. They've been looking for rustlers. I've been losing stock for a while now. Maybe up to two hundred head, all told. Like I said, we've spent a lot of time lately looking for the rustlers, but we ain't had no luck at all so far, and we've seen no sign of your father.'

'I suppose it's just possible,' he went on, 'that your father met up with some Comanches. I know for sure that a raiding party's been seen between here and the New Mexico border.'

'I guess it's possible,' said Jack. 'But if Comanches killed him, his body will be lying out there somewhere. I'll just carry on looking for him.'

During his conversation with him, Jack hadn't taken to Weaver. He was too smooth, and there was a ruthless look about him. And Jack had the feeling that the rancher was hiding something. He got up to leave. As he left the house with Weaver, he saw a lean man, with a drooping moustache, walk from the bunkhouse towards the cookshack.

'That's my foreman, Walt Stringer,' said Weaver. 'He's the one who made sure that the hands kept a lookout for your father.'

Weaver watched Jack as he rode off. Stringer walked over from the cookshack to join him, as Jack was disappearing from view.

'That's the son of the man we hanged, Walt,' said Weaver. 'I still reckon we can't be blamed for hanging him, the way things looked, but if word gets round that we hanged an innocent man, we'll be in real trouble with the law. D'you reckon that the men who saw the hanging will all keep their mouths shut?'

'They all know now,' replied Stringer, 'that the man we hanged was a rancher from Colorado, and I reckon I've convinced them that keeping quiet about it is the only sensible thing to do. I've told them again not to say anything about it to the cook, and the hands who weren't there when it happened.

'What d'you reckon Kilgour will do now?' he went on.

'He says he's going to carry on looking,'

45

replied Weaver. 'But when he doesn't find a body anywhere, I reckon it won't be all that long before he gives up, and heads back to Colorado.'

'I hope so,' said Stringer. 'It sure makes me nervous, him nosing around here.'

Jack continued his search that day, and the following one, without success. He was just making camp for the second night after leaving Weaver, when a prospector rode up, on a mule, with a burro packed with gear trailing behind him. He was a small, elderly man, deeply tanned, and bearded. He looked at Jack with a tentative smile on his face.

'Howdy,' he said. 'Mind if I keep you company for the night? I'm a mite tired of talking to nothing but a mule and a burro and myself for the last few months. My name's Price, Hank Price.'

'Light down,' said Jack. 'Glad of your company.'

Price dismounted, unpacked the burro, and watered the mule and burro at the stream nearby. When he had done this, he sat down at the camp fire for a meal, with Jack. He told Jack that he had been prospecting through The Indian Territory, and the Texas Panhandle, and that he was now heading for Colorado, to try his luck there.

'Have you been in this area for a while?' Jack asked him.

'Around two months,' replied Price. 'In some hilly country east of here. Didn't have no luck, though.'

Jack explained to Price what he himself was doing in the area. He described his father and his horse, and he asked Price if he had seen any sign of either of them.

'I might have,' said Price, reflectively, and paused.

Jack stared at him. 'Carry on,' he said. 'If you know anything at all that might help, I'd sure like to hear about it.'

'Well,' said Price. 'Two or three weeks ago, I was standing just inside the entrance to a small ravine, pretty well due east of where we are now. It's maybe sixty miles from here. The mule and burro were grazing well up the ravine. I spotted five riders, and some cattle, coming from the west, and dodged out of sight, in a patch of brush, before they saw me. I watched them from cover. They passed close by the ravine. They were driving a small herd, maybe two hundred head.

'I got a good look,' he went on, 'at the nearest rider to me, on one flank of the herd. He was a dark-skinned man, with a pock-marked face, riding a pinto. He had a scar of some sort on his cheek. The rider on the other side of the herd was a tall, slim man, on a big white horse. It was a horse that really took the eye. As for the other three riders, I didn't see anything special about them.'

'And what sort of hat was the man on the white horse wearing?' asked Jack.

'I could see it plain,' replied Price. 'It was a Texas hat, all white, like the horse.'

'That sounds like my father,' said Jack. 'Did it look like he was a prisoner?'

'It's hard to say,' replied Price. 'He was riding alone, on the flank, but there was another rider not far behind him. If he was a prisoner, and tried to run off, they could easily have gunned him down.

'But there was something that struck me about that bunch,' Price went on. 'They didn't look like no cowhands to me, and they were heading away from the JW range. I figured that maybe those cattle were stolen, and they were taking them up to Kansas.'

'If they *were* rustlers,' said Jack, 'I just can't figure what my father was doing with them.'

He thought hard for a few moments, then spoke again.

'I suppose it's just possible,' he went on, 'that he stumbled on them while they were stealing cattle, and they got the drop on him. They couldn't leave him behind alive, to put the law on their trail, so they took him along. Maybe they figured to set him loose after they sold the herd.'

'That's a big "maybe",' said Price. 'I don't like saying it, but if that *was* your father I saw, his chances of staying alive long can't be all that good.'

'You're right,' said Jack. 'I don't see no point in looking around here any more. I'll head for that place where you saw the man on the white horse, and carry on from there. Maybe you could tell me exactly where that ravine is.'

# FOUR

Jack picked up the tracks of the cattle outside the ravine from which Price had seen the rustlers. The tracks, still fairly clear, were heading due east, and as far as Jack could tell, they tallied roughly with the size of the herd that Price had seen. He saw no sign of any other herds being driven in the direction he was following.

He followed the tracks for the next two days, during which they veered slightly north, and finally crossed into The Indian Territory. About thirty miles further on, the tracks were lost where they met the Western Cattle Trail, over which many thousands of cattle had been driven from Texas to Dodge City, Kansas, also further north to the Wyoming, Montana, Nebraska and Dakota Territories.

Jack followed the Western Trail northward, across the North Canadian and Cimarron Rivers, and on to Dodge City, where he arrived late in the afternoon. He decided to stay on in Dodge City for a while, in the hope that he might find some trace there of his father, or the rustlers. He could think of nothing else that he might do. He was painfully aware that he was not even sure that the man on the white horse *was* his father, and that, of the other four men seen, Price had only been able to describe one in any detail.

Jack took a room at Widow Tillman's boarding house on main street, close to a couple of saloons. From his room window, he could see much of what was going on in the centre of town. Mrs Tillman was a cheerful, bustling, amply-proportioned lady, with a reputation for providing her guests with meals of reasonable quality, and a comfortable room.

After taking a meal, Jack took his horse over to a livery stable just along the street, and led it inside. The liveryman, Will Drury, was busy doing something at the back of the stable. He was a small, pleasant-looking man, in his forties. He smiled, as he walked up to Jack. Jack noticed that he was walking awkwardly, as if one of his legs had been damaged.

'Howdy,' said the liveryman.

'Howdy,' said Jack. 'You got room for my horse?'

'Only just,' said Drury. 'You aiming to stay long?'

'Can't say,' replied Jack. 'I've just rode in, and I'm hoping I'll find somebody who probably got here a few weeks ago. He's a tall man, bearded, riding a big white gelding, and wearing a white Texas hat. He might have another man with him, a dark-skinned man, with a pock-marked face, and a V-shaped scar on his cheek. Don't suppose you've seen either of them around just lately?'

The liveryman thought hard for a short while, then replied.

'Can't say I have,' he said. 'There are a few white horses around, but they all belong to people living here permanent.'

Jack looked around the stable. Most of the stalls were occupied.

'Looks like you're busy just now,' he said.

'I sure am,' said Drury. 'We've had a lot of drives in lately, from Texas, and there's a lot of cattlemen and buyers around. I can tell you, I'm near run off my feet, and help is hard to find. And this busted leg of mine don't make things any easier. Fell off a horse a couple of years ago when a cinch broke, and that leg never mended right. It just ain't much use at all.'

'S'long as I'm here, just waiting for those men I told you about, I could lend a hand if you like,' offered Jack. 'I like horses, and it'd give me something to do while I'm waiting. But I might have to leave the job pretty quick, when the time comes.'

'I'm going to take you up on that offer,' said Drury. 'And thanks. I like horses myself. That's why I'm doing this job. The name's Drury, Will Drury, by the way.'

'Jack Kilgour,' said Jack. 'I'll start in the morning.'

He went to the boarding house, and lay down in his room. He was tired after a long day's ride.

In the livery stable the next day, he found that he got on well with Drury, and his wages more than paid for his room and board. During his time off each day, he had a walk around town, looking for any sign of the two men he was searching for.

It was mid-afternoon, three days after he had started work at the stable, when two trail-hands came in for their horses. Both men were wearing six-guns. Jack, working at the back of the stable, could see that one of them, a big man, florid-faced, was a little the worse for liquor. His companion, a smaller man, was grinning, as Drury handed the horses over to them.

'Ain't got much of a head for liquor, have you, Wilson?' he said. 'You think you can stay on that horse?'

Wilson cursed. 'You've got a big mouth, Jones,' he said. 'The horse ain't been born yet I can't ride, drunk or sober.'

As the two men walked their horses outside, Drury followed them. Both the men mounted, the big man's mount rearing a little as he hit the saddle. He quirted the horse hard, and in retaliation, it bucked and reared, and deposited him on the ground, his shoulder and head hitting the ground hard. Drury took the reins of the horse, and it stood quietly, a few yards away from Wilson.

Wilson lay still for a moment. Then he shook his head, got up, walked over and took the reins from Drury, and walked unsteadily to a nearby hitching-rail. He fastened the reins securely to the rail. Then he walked back from the rail, turned, and standing at the side of the horse, he raised his quirt high, with the obvious intention of striking it on the haunch. His face was distorted with rage.

'No!' shouted Drury, limping as quickly as he could towards Wilson, and grabbing the lash of the quirt before Wilson had directed it towards the horse. Jack, hearing the commotion outside, quickly buckled on his gunbelt, and ran out of the stable, just in time to see Wilson punch Drury hard in the face, and push him so that his weight came down on his crippled leg, and he fell to the ground. Standing over Drury, Wilson raised his quirt to strike the liveryman.

Jack ran up to Wilson, grabbed the hand holding the quirt, and pulled the trail-hand away from Drury. Then, before Wilson could recover his balance, Jack delivered two powerful punches to the pit of Wilson's stomach, followed immediately by one jolting knock-out punch to the side of his jaw.

As Wilson fell, Jack, out of the corner of his eye, saw Jones starting to reach for his gun. Turning fast, he pulled his own gun, and lined it up on Jones, just as the muzzle of the trail-hand's gun was clearing the holster.

'I wouldn't,' said Jack.

Seeing Jack's levelled gun, Jones froze.

'Drop it in the holster,' ordered Jack.

Jones complied, then looked down at Wilson, who was starting to stir.

'I don't hold with what Wilson was doing

to that horse,' he said, 'but he's my partner. That's why I started to take a hand.'

Ignoring him, Jack helped Drury to his feet.

'You OK?' he asked. Drury nodded.

Jack spoke to Jones.

'You'd better go,' he said. 'Both of you.'

Jones helped Wilson to his feet, then on to his horse. Then he mounted his own horse, and the two men rode off. As they did so, Drury turned to Jack.

'Jack,' he said. 'Thanks for helping me out. But where in blazes did you learn to pull a gun like that? I've seen a few gunfights in Dodge, but I've never seen a gun slide out of a holster quicker'n yours did just now.'

'I reckon it's just a knack I've got,' replied Jack. 'And a bit of practice helps, of course.'

Later that day, Jack told Drury about his father's disappearance, and the real reason for his own presence in Dodge.

'You sure must be worried,' said Drury, 'not knowing whether your father's dead or alive.'

'That's the worst of it,' said Jack, 'but there's nothing else I can do but wait here for a while, to see if something turns up.'

When he finished work later, Jack went to the Telegraph Office, to send a telegram to

Jim Morgan at the Diamond K Ranch, asking Jim to let him know in Dodge if he got any news of Joe Kilgour.

Two days later, Jack was in the stable alone, sweeping the floor, when the trail-hand Jones walked in. Jack stiffened, but Jones just stood in front of him, shuffling his feet, and looking embarrassed.

'I'm heading back for Texas today,' he said, 'with some of the other trail-hands. I just dropped in to thank you for the other day. The way you handle a gun, I'm pretty sure you could have wounded me, or finished me off, if you'd had a mind to. I'm sorry the liveryman got knocked around like that. Maybe you'll tell him that.'

'I'll do that,' said Jack, then a thought struck him, as Jones was turning to leave.

'Say,' he said. 'Maybe you can help me. Did you bring cattle up the Western Trail?'

'Sure did,' replied Jones. 'We got here a week ago.'

'Somewhere near the Cimarron River,' asked Jack, 'did you pick up some more cattle?'

Jones stared at Jack.

'How did you know that?' he asked. 'There were about two hundred head. They were grazing just back from the main trail

57

south of the river, when we reached the bed-ground for the night. There were five men with them. One of them rode up to the trail boss, and they talked for a while. Then the trail boss counted the cattle, while they were driven to join the main herd. I had the feeling that the trail boss knew that the cattle would be waiting there when he arrived.'

'Did you notice the brand on those cattle?' asked Jack.

'Yes,' replied Jones. 'It was "JWT", I think. In fact, I'm pretty sure of it.'

Jack was now sure that the cattle had come from the JW Ranch. With the help of a running iron, the addition of a 'T' to the brand would have been a simple matter.

'Did you get a good look at the five men with the cattle?' asked Jack.

'Yes,' replied Jones. 'They took supper with us, and stayed the night. They took off next morning, heading east.'

'Did one of the men have a pock-marked face, and a V-shaped scar on his cheek?' asked Jack.

'Yes,' replied Jones. 'I was chatting with him over supper. He said his name was Barrett, Clem Barrett, and I think he said his boss was called Duggan. We were talking about Dodge. He said he was heading east, further into The Indian Territory, for a spell, then he was going to visit Dodge.'

'Did you notice his horse?' asked Jack.

'I did,' replied Jones. 'It was a pinto.'

'Did one of the men ride a big white horse, with a black patch on its tail?' asked Jack.

'Yes,' replied Jones. 'I had a good look at that horse. I sure would be proud to own it.'

'Did you see a brand on the horse?' asked Jack.

'There *was* a brand,' replied Jones. 'I don't remember exactly what it was, but I think it was a letter inside a diamond.'

'Did the owner of the horse have a full head of hair?' asked Jack.

'Hardly,' replied Jones. 'Once, when he lifted his hat for a few seconds, I noticed he had a bald patch right on the top of his head.'

'The other three men,' asked Jack. 'Were any of them around the six foot mark?'

'No,' replied Jones. 'They were all around average height, maybe a bit less.'

Jack thanked Jones for the information, and the trail-hand departed. Jack knew for certain now, that his father was not one of the five men who had driven the rustled cattle from the Panhandle. He was also reasonably sure that the white gelding was the one his father was riding when he disappeared. He decided to stay on in Dodge, in the hope that Barrett showed up. When Drury came in, a little later, Jack told him about the information he had just received from Jones.

'What d'you do now?' asked Drury.

'I've got to find out what's happened to my father,' replied Jack. 'And I'm pretty sure that those five rustlers might have the answer. I don't have any other lead, so I've got to find them. So I'll watch out for Barrett, and if he does turn up, maybe he'll lead me to the others.'

Just then, Andrew Brennan, editor and proprietor of the 'Dodge Messenger' walked into the stable, and Jack went for his horse. Brennan was a lean, spry, often feisty man, in his seventies, with a grey moustache. He wore a pair of glasses, without which he was virtually blind.

Brennan was a fairly frequent visitor to the stable. He called for his horse almost every day, to ride out either for pleasure, or on a quest for news, and Jack usually chatted with him for a few minutes before he left. During these talks, Brennan was constantly quoting examples of the unruly behaviour of the visiting trail-hands, and bemoaning the inability, or unwillingness, of the law officers of Dodge to put a stop to it. These views were also forcibly expressed, regularly, in the front page editorials in his paper.

Brennan returned from his ride about two hours later, and handed his horse over to Jack, telling him he was going to do some work on the paper. He asked Jack if he would call in later on, for a few minutes, to help him move some heavy equipment around. Leaving the stable, Brennan walked along the street to the small wooden building just past the hotel, where he produced his newspaper. He sat at his desk, and started to work on his next front-page editorial.

He had been hard at it for fifteen minutes, shouting to himself, and occasionally punching his fist in the air, when two trail-hands called Tipton and Spicer pushed the door open, and walked inside. One of them walked over to the window, and pulled the blind down. Then they both walked up to Brennan, and stood looking down at him.

'What d'you want?' asked Brennan, sharply.

'Just a friendly talk,' replied Tipton, a big man, with an unshaven face, and several missing teeth. 'Our trail boss ain't too pleased about all those things you keep saying about trail-hands in that paper of yours. He reckons a trail-hand's entitled to a bit of fun after four months in the saddle.'

Brennan bridled. He could smell whisky on the breaths of the two men.

'If that's how he feels, why don't he come and see me himself?' he asked, 'and I'd tell him that nobody minds the trail-hands enjoying themselves in the gambling houses and saloons, and shooting each other down in there, if that's what they want. What we ain't going to put up with is drunken cowboys riding round the streets of Dodge, and shooting up the town, and putting the lives of innocent citizens at risk. And until it's stopped by the law, that's what I'll keep on saying in my paper.'

Tipton walked round the desk, pulled the editor's swivel chair round, and slapped Brennan hard, first on one side of the face, then the other, before the editor could defend himself. Spicer walked behind Brennan, and held his arms.

'Maybe we can change your mind,' said Tipton, pulling off Brennan's glasses, dropping them on the floor, and stamping on them several times, with his heel. Then, taking hold of the front of Brennan's collar, he yanked him out of his chair, and on to his feet, with Spicer still holding on to the editor's arms. Then, with a large open hand, Tipton systematically, and with considerable force, slapped each side of Brennan's face alternately, until the blood started to flow down the old man's cheeks, and from his nostrils.

Jack pushed the door open, and walked in, just as Tipton was pausing for breath. He saw the blood on Brennan's face. Tipton turned his head, and the look on Jack's face sent him reaching for his gun. Spicer did the same, but a little later than his partner.

Jack easily beat Tipton to the draw, and shot him in the right shoulder. The trailhand's gun fell to the floor. Spicer's gun snagged in the holster, and in his haste, he fired it before it was properly lined up on Jack, and his shot missed its target. Jack had time to place a bullet in the fleshy part of Spicer's upper arm. Spicer's gun fell to the floor. Jack held his Peacemaker on the two men, while picking up their guns.

Brennan who had collapsed on the floor as Jack came in, caught hold of the edge of the desk, and slowly pulled himself up, with Jack's help, and sat on the chair. Holding a handkerchief to his bleeding nose, he shook his head from side to side.

'You all right?' asked Jack.

Brennan stopped shaking his head. 'I'm all right,' he replied. 'I'm sure glad you showed up. Don't know how far they meant to go. Let's take them along to the marshal.'

He groped on the floor for his glasses, saw that they were beyond repair, and took another pair from his desk drawer, and put them on.

Holding his Peacemaker, Jack prodded the two men through the door, and through the small crowd which had gathered outside at the sound of gunfire. He told them to walk to the Marshal's Office, down at the far end of the street. When they walked in, they found the marshal seated at his desk. He looked up as they entered, and his eyes widened as he saw Brennan's battered face, and the two wounded men.

'These two men,' said Brennan, 'came into my place, and assaulted me. Seems like their trail boss didn't like what I said in my paper about trail-hands shooting up the town, and suchlike. It was lucky for me that Kilgour here happened by when he did.'

The marshal looked at Jack, as he laid the trail-hands' guns on the desk. The lawman pointed to Tipton and Spicer.

'You shoot these two?' he asked.

'I did,' replied Jack. 'Lucky for them I had time to plant those bullets where I did. You can see those wounds ain't too bad.'

The marshal gave Jack a long, hard look. Then he took the two men into the cells. When he returned, he had a closer look at Brennan's face.

'You'd better go see the doctor,' he said. 'And when he's finished with you, tell him to come and see to these two men in the cells.'

# FIVE

Three weeks passed uneventfully, and Jack was growing increasingly frustrated, until late on a Saturday afternoon, a rider stopped outside the livery stable, dismounted from the pinto he was riding, and stood outside the stable door.

Jack, working in the dim light at the back of the stable, looked up, and seeing the pinto, he looked hard at the man holding its reins. He could see that the man was of medium height, and the pockmarks and the scar on his face were clearly visible. Jack was sure he was looking at Barrett, one of the men who might be able to provide the answer to his father's disappearance.

Quickly, he walked out of the back door of the stable, and into the rear of Drury's house, unseen by Barrett. He told Drury who the man outside was, and asked him to attend to the rustler. He himself stayed in the house. Drury went out, and walked over to Barrett.

'This horse has gone a bit lame,' Barrett

said. 'Needs a rest, I reckon, and maybe a new set of shoes. You got a horse here I could hire for two days? I want to ride north to Brent first thing tomorrow, and back here on Monday morning. I'll pick up the pinto around eleven.'

'I've got a horse you can have,' said Drury, 'and I'll take a look at those shoes for you, and get them changed, if it's needed.'

'Right,' said Barrett. 'What I need right now, is some food, and then a good night's sleep. See you in the morning.' He headed for the hotel, and disappeared inside.

Drury went into the house, and told Jack of Barrett's plans.

'I don't want him to see me while he's in town,' said Jack, 'so I'll stay out of his way. And I'll follow him when he leaves on Monday. I'm hoping he'll lead me to the rest of the gang. I've got a feeling they're holed up south of here somewhere.'

The following day, after Barrett had left town, Jack rode out of Dodge, on the trail leading to Ellsworth, for a private session of gun-handling and target practice. He carried a small sack of tin cans with him. About four miles out of Dodge, Jack left the trail, just before it passed through a small ravine, and rode up to some high ground, then into a hollow out of sight of the trail. He dismounted, and sat for a while, checking that his Peacemaker and rifle were in order. Then, using the tin cans he had brought with him, he had some target practice.

It was a pleasant afternoon. The sun was shining, but not too hot. After he had finished shooting, he ate some food he had brought with him, then laid down, and dozed for a time. When he awoke, he got up, and walked to the rim of the hollow, and looked down along the trail. There was no one in sight. He was just turning to go to his horse, when he caught sight of a horse standing at the top of the wall of the ravine through which the trail passed. Then he saw a man close to the horse. The man and horse were standing behind a rock, and the man, with a rifle in his hand, was looking along the trail towards Dodge. Jack looked along the trail again, and saw that a rider had just come in sight.

Looking back at the man and horse standing behind the rock, Jack thought that the horse, a chestnut, looked as if it belonged to an unsavoury character called Jake Parminter, who worked for Darrell Ranger, owner of the Alhambra Saloon in Dodge. He was sure of this, when the man turned his head, so that his face was visible to Jack.

Looking once again along the trail from Dodge, Jack could now see that the rider, who was approaching at a canter, was a gambler called Dale Prescott. Jack had seen him once or twice playing poker in the saloon, and he recognized him by his horse, a handsome black, and the distinctive clothes he was wearing – a completely black outfit, relieved only by a colourful bandanna.

As Prescott approached the entrance to the ravine, Parminter stood up, and aimed his rifle over the top of the rock, at the rider below. Before he could pull the trigger, Jack, who had already taken aim at a point near the top of the rock close to Parminter's face, fired his rifle. As the bullet struck the rock close to his right cheek, spattered his face with small fragments of rock, and ricocheted off, Parminter jerked sideways, lost his footing, and fell down the sloping wall of the ravine, in full view of Prescott.

When Parminter hit the bottom of the ravine, he rolled over once, and was just reaching for his gun, when he saw the revolver in Prescott's hand. He lay still, groaning.

Jack quickly ran to the place where Parminter had disappeared from view. Cautiously, he looked down into the ravine, and then, from cover, he called down to Prescott below. The gambler had dismounted and had taken Parminter's gun.

'Hold your fire, Prescott,' Jack shouted. 'I'm coming down.'

He climbed slowly down the side of the ravine, while the gambler kept him covered. He reached the bottom, and walked up to Prescott. The gambler was a little over average height, and in his early thirties, clean-shaven, with black hair, cut short. He looked closely at Jack, then tucked Parminter's gun into his belt.

'I've seen you around in Dodge,' he said. 'In the livery stable?'

Jack nodded. 'Kilgour's the name,' he said.

'What's been going on here?' asked Prescott.

'I saw Parminter waiting for you up there, with a rifle,' said Jack. 'I could see he was ready to fire at you, so I sent a bullet just past his face, into the rock he was leaning against. Never saw a man jump so much. In fact, he jumped so far sideways, he fell down into the ravine.'

'Well, well,' said Prescott, turning to Parminter. 'I see it all now. Your boss Ranger must have sent you. I could see he was

70

pretty riled when I hit that winning streak at poker last night, and took a lot of his money away from him. He must've heard I was leaving for Ellsworth today, so he sent you ahead to bushwack me, and get the money back. He ain't going to like it Parminter, when you end up in jail.'

Parminter cursed. He was holding his right arm.

'My arm's broke,' he groaned.

Jack walked up to him, and felt the arm.

'Looks like he's right,' he said to Prescott. 'I'll get him back to town. I'll go get my horse, and Parminter's too.'

'Kilgour,' said Prescott. 'I'm mighty beholden to you. If it hadn't been for you, likely I'd be a dead man by now. I'd no notion I was heading into an ambush.'

'Glad I was around,' said Jack. 'I'll go get those horses.'

'Right,' said Prescott. 'I'll wait here, and keep an eye on Parminter. And I'll ride back to Dodge with you. I've just got to see Ranger's face, when we bring Parminter in. I figure we'd better take him straight to the Marshal's Office. Likely the marshal will want to pick up Ranger, when we tell him what's happened.'

When they got back to Dodge, after a

painful ride for Parminter, they took their prisoner to the Marshal's Office, and told the deputy marshal inside what had happened. He put Parminter into a cell, and sent for a doctor to see to his broken arm. Then he asked Jack and Prescott to call in and see the marshal the following morning, when he was expected back in town.

While Jack went back to the livery stable, Prescott walked along to the Alhambra Saloon, and went inside. Ranger was sitting at a table, playing poker with three other men. They looked like cattlemen to Prescott. Ranger's eyes widened, as he looked up, and saw Prescott walking towards him. The gambler stopped on the other side of the table, facing Ranger.

'Surprised to see me, Ranger?' he asked. 'I figured you for a bad loser, but I never thought you'd go so far as to kill a man to get your money back. Parminter fell down on the job. He's in jail with a broken arm, and when the marshal gets back, he'll be paying you a visit.'

Ranger looked up at Prescott. His cold impassive look concealed the intense anger inside him.

'When I speak to the marshal,' he said, 'I'm sure I can convince him that if Parminter did attempt to kill you – and you've still got to prove that – I had nothing to do with it. Parminter must have been holding a grudge against you for some reason.'

'We'll see,' said Prescott. 'So happens I have a witness to the murder attempt, and maybe Parminter'll decide it's in his best interests to tell the marshal you put him up to it.'

As Prescott left, Ranger watched him go, and for a brief moment, there was murder in his eyes. Then, excusing himself, he abruptly left the table, and went upstairs to his room, beckoning one of his men to follow him.

The following morning, Prescott went along to the Marshal's Office. The marshal was inside.

'The deputy passed on what you told him,' said the marshal, 'so there ain't no need to go over it again. There won't be no trial. Parminter was shot and killed in the jail, during the night. Looks like somebody called him to the cell window, and shot him through the bars. We don't know who did it.'

'I think I can guess, marshal,' said Prescott. 'Ranger must have done it. He was scared Parminter would let out that he had ordered the killing.'

'You'd better be careful what you say, Prescott,' warned the marshal. 'I happen to know that Ranger was in his saloon, sitting at a card table, when Parminter was shot.'

'You don't think he'd be such a fool as to do the shooting himself, do you marshal?' asked Prescott. 'He'd get one of his men to do it.'

'I'm warning you again, Prescott,' said the marshal. 'It ain't healthy, shooting your mouth off like that. We don't want your sort in Dodge. I'm telling you to get out of town. You've got till tomorrow noon, to leave.'

'So it's like that, is it?' asked Prescott, having heard rumours that the marshal's income was supplemented by handsome contributions from the saloon owners in Dodge, in return for him turning a blind eye on the dubious methods they sometimes employed to extract money from their patrons.

The marshal's face reddened.

'Leave by noon tomorrow,' he said, 'or you'll be sorry.'

Prescott left, and walked along to the livery stable, to tell Jack what had happened. Jack was out, and not due back for a while, so the gambler chatted for a while with Drury. He was just about to leave, when Jack came in, and Drury left.

'When do we set off?' asked Prescott.

'Set off where?' asked Jack.

'Why, on the trail of this man Barrett, of course,' replied Prescott.

'You've been talking to Drury,' said Jack.

'That's right,' said Prescott. 'And it's clear to me that you're liable to come up against five rustlers or more. The odds against you are too high. It so happens I've been getting a bit bored with gambling lately, and I figured a bit of excitement would perk me up. That's why I want to go along with you.'

'Just because I managed to stop Parminter shooting you,' said Jack, 'ain't no reason for you to get mixed up in this business.'

'My mind's made up,' said Prescott, 'and seeing as we're going to be partners, you can call me Dale.'

'It's a fact,' said Jack, who had taken a liking to the gambler, 'that I could do with some help. If you're set on coming, I'll be glad to have you along. The name is Jack.'

He spent the next twenty minutes telling Dale exactly what action he himself had taken since his father went missing. Then he moved towards the door, as Drury came in.

'I'm going out now to see if Brennan, the editor of the "Messenger" is in his office,'

Jack told Dale. 'You'd better come along with me.'

They found Brennan working on the next edition of the paper. He stopped and listened, as Jack explained what he wanted. When Jack and Dale left him, ninety minutes later, Jack was carrying a small poster, which he folded and crumpled, and rubbed gently with some dust off the street, to disguise its newness. Before they parted company, Jack told Dale that Barrett would be picking up his pinto around eleven the following morning.

'We don't want Barrett to see either of us,' he said, 'so come over early, and we'll wait in Drury's house till he's gone. And bring a sack of provisions with you. We may be camping out for a while.'

'Right,' said Dale. 'And I'll be wearing cowboy clothes in the morning.'

The next morning, Drury waited in the stable for Barrett to arrive. He turned up a few minutes before eleven, and handed over the rented horse. Drury brought the pinto out of its stall, and saddled it. Barrett paid the bill, and left. Drury went back into his house.

'We'll be leaving soon,' Jack told the liveryman, as they watched Barrett ride off down the street, heading south out of town.

'Both of you?' asked Drury, looking at Dale.

Jack nodded, and smiled. 'I just can't get it into his thick head that it ain't going to be no picnic,' he said.

'When I told your story to Dale here,' said Drury, 'I was hoping he'd lend a hand. Good luck to the both of you.'

# SIX

Jack and Dale took their leave of Drury, and headed out of town on Barrett's trail. Jack was carrying with him field-glasses belonging to his father, which he had picked up at the Diamond K, when leaving to search for the missing rancher.

Using the glasses, they kept Barrett in sight, while keeping a good distance behind him. He was heading roughly south-east, parallel to the nearby Chisholm Cattle Trail, which ran from South Texas, across The Indian Territory, to the cattle towns of Kansas.

Barrett had ridden about fifteen miles from Dodge, when he turned east, and headed for some broken ground about a mile ahead. Jack and Dale stopped, and from the shelter of a small copse, Jack watched the rustler through the glasses. He saw Barrett ride through the entrance to a small ravine, and disappear from view. He watched through the glasses for half an hour. He could see further up the ravine, but there was no sign of Barrett there, nor at the entrance.

'I guess maybe he's met the others there,' he said to Dale. 'We'll wait here for a couple of hours or so, then we'll ride on so's to reach the ravine just before dark. That way, they won't suspect we've been following Barrett. What I plan to do is ride in on them casual-like, and see how things develop. Maybe we can persuade them to let us join the gang. If we can do that, maybe they'll let something slip about what happened to my father.

'And don't forget our new name is Kincaid,' he went on, 'and you're my brother.'

He paused, then continued.

'It could be a dangerous business,' he said. 'Now's the time to back out, if you're having second thoughts.'

Dale smiled. 'It's just starting to get interesting,' he said. 'Why should I let you hog all the excitement?'

Jack smiled back at him. 'That gun of yours,' he said. 'You can handle it OK?'

Dale made a draw, fast enough to impress Jack, then he rapidly spun his gun forward half a dozen times, then backward the same number of times, then, after letting the gun handle slap into the palm of his hand, he returned the gun quickly and smoothly to its holster.

'Yes, but can you hit anything?' asked Jack.

He avoided Dale's playful blow, and turned the glasses on to the ravine again.

The sun was low in the sky when they left their cover. As they approached the ravine, they made no attempt to hide, and as they reached the narrow entrance, and passed through, walking their horses, they were speaking loudly to one another.

They continued slowly up the ravine, still talking, and rounded a bend. Ahead of them, about fifty yards away, was a smoking camp fire, with six men seated around it, all wearing guns. In the background were six horses, on a picket line. One of the horses was a big white.

One of the men saw them, and his hand dropped to his gun handle. He said something to the others, and they all tensed, and stared at Jack and Dale. Two of them slowly stood up, their hands on their gun handles. Jack recognized one of them as Barrett. The other was Duggan, the leader of the gang.

They rode up to the rustlers, and stopped their horses. Jack raised his arm in greeting.

'Howdy,' he said.

'Who're you?' asked Duggan.

'Name's Jack Kincaid,' replied Jack, 'and this is my brother Dale.'

'What're you doing in these parts?' asked Duggan, suspiciously.

'Heading back to Texas,' replied Jack. 'We helped to bring a trail herd up to Dodge. Got there two weeks ago. Spent all our money, and now we're on our way back home. Saw the smoke from your camp fire, and had a hankering for some company. You mind if we stay here for the night?'

Duggan pulled his gun, and Barrett followed suit. They covered Jack and Dale. Duggan told them to dismount, and stand in front of their horses, with their hands up.

'You're a smooth talker, stranger,' said Duggan to Jack, when they had complied. 'Might be you're lawmen'.

'Hell, no,' said Jack. 'I take that as an insult. Lawmen and me ain't exactly friends. 'Specially when they kicked us out of Dodge for no reason at all.'

'Clem,' said Duggan. 'Take these mens' guns, then go through their pockets and saddlebags. Maybe there's something there that'll tell us just who they are. They don't look like no trail-hands to me.'

Barrett walked up to Jack and Dale, pulled out their guns, and threw them down out of reach. Then he searched their pockets, finding a small wad of banknotes in Jack's pocket, and the same in Dale's. He handed these to Duggan. Then he looked at the contents of the saddlebags, and out of Jack's he pulled a folded poster, dirty and crumpled. It was the same poster that Brennan had printed for Jack in Dodge.

Barrett unfolded the poster, glanced at it, and immediately handed it to Duggan. Duggan studied it closely. There were two printed likenesses at the top of the poster, bearing a passable resemblance to Jack and Dale. Underneath the likenesses, the poster read:

'STATE OF MISSOURI
REWARDS FOR THE ARREST OF
BANK AND TRAIN ROBBERS

Whereas JACK KINCAID and DALE KINCAID have together committed robbery within this State, a reward of eight hundred dollars is offered for the arrest and conviction of each of the above.'

Duggan finished reading the notice, then looked at Jack and Dale, and back to the faces at the top of the poster. He handed the poster to Barrett, and looked at Jack and Dale again.

'Well, well,' he said. 'It seems that what you've just told us is a pack of lies. What's to stop us handing you over to the nearest lawman, so's we can claim that sixteen hundred dollars reward?'

Jack looked round the group.

'I was a fool to keep that poster,' he said, 'but I'm asking myself what a bunch of men like yourselves is doing, hiding in this ravine, close to The Indian Territory. You sure ain't ordinary ranch-hands. I've got a feeling that you can't hand us over to the law, because you're hiding from the law yourselves.

'It so happens,' he went on, 'that we had to leave Missouri in a hurry, because we had a posse too close on our tail after the last bank raid we pulled there. We figured it might be a good idea to move west, and set up in business again where we ain't known. Maybe we could join up with you boys? There ain't much we don't know about robbing banks and trains. And we've done the odd stagecoach robbery now and then. And we helped the James boys out a couple of times, as well.'

Duggan took the poster back from

Barrett, and studied it again.

'You've sure got a nerve,' he said, 'asking to join up with us, but it just happens we've got a big job on hand, and I could use a couple more men. We've done some rustling lately, for the first time, but it's hard work, and not much to show for it, so we're back to robbing banks and stagecoaches again. Just now, we're figuring to rob a bank in Hays.'

He handed back the wanted poster and the banknotes to Jack and Dale.

'Pick up your guns,' he said.

When they had done this, he continued speaking.

'Clem here,' he said, pointing to Barrett, 'has just got back with news, from a contact of ours, that a big consignment of gold and banknotes is due to be delivered to the bank exactly one week from today. There should be enough to make us all rich. Are you interested in helping us out?'

Jack and Dale both nodded.

'We sure are,' replied Jack. 'It was a real stroke of luck meeting up with you boys.'

'Right,' said Duggan. 'Tie your horses on that picket line. Then we'll have a talk.'

Jack walked his horse over to the line, and tied it next to the big white horse standing there. Hidden from view between the two horses, he bent down to look closely at the brand on the flank of the white. A crude attempt had been made to alter the markings, but the original Diamond K brand was still decipherable. Jack was certain, without any doubt, that this was the horse his father had left home on. He looked across the back of his horse at Dale, who was watching him, and nodded. Then they walked back to the fire, and sat down with Duggan and his men.

'There's one thing to make clear to you Kincaids right away,' said Duggan. 'This outfit only has one boss. If you come in with us, you've got to obey my orders.'

'That goes without saying,' said Jack. 'One gang, one boss. It's the only way.'

'Right, then,' said the gang leader. 'My name's Duggan. And this is Clem Barrett.' He pointed to the man with the pockmarked face. 'And over there is Frank Moore, and Dave Taylor, and Mort Gilbert.' He pointed to the three men in turn. They were all, like Barrett, around average height and build. Gilbert, though still in his thirties, was almost bald. The three men nodded.

'And the man on the other side of the fire,' he went on, 'is Brad Manton. He's only just joined up with us.'

Manton was a small stocky man, with a moustache. He nodded to Jack and Dale.

'You boys any good with those forty-fives?' asked Duggan.

'I figure we can hold our own,' replied Jack.

'Not that we go out with the idea of killing anybody,' said Duggan. 'But now and again, there's some fool wants to be a hero, and there ain't nothing to do but finish him off.'

'You heading for Hays soon?' asked Jack.

'In about five days' time,' replied Duggan. 'I've got to find a place a few miles out of town, where we can hole up without being seen. And when we get there, I want you two to ride into town, and give the bank a good looking-over. None of us has ever been inside it, and we ain't too keen on any of us riding into Hays ourselves before the robbery, because we know the marshal has wanted posters on all of us. But it ain't likely anybody there'll recognize you two, you being new to these parts.

'What we know about the bank is just hearsay,' he went on, 'but we know there's usually the president and a cashier working inside, and there's a vault behind the counter. So we'll empty the cash drawer, and take what we want from the vault.'

'Sounds good,' said Jack. Then he embarked on an imaginary, and highly-coloured account of a bank raid in Missouri, in which he and Dale had participated, along with the James brothers. Then he turned the conversation to rustling.

'This rustling business,' he said. 'It's something we know nothing about. You say it ain't so profitable nowadays?'

'That's right,' said Duggan. 'Time was when there was plenty of money to be made in rustling, 'most anywhere in cattle country. But the ranchers keep a lot closer watch on their cattle nowadays. And if you gets caught red-handed, you're liable to be left hanging from the nearest tree. The good times are over.

'I reckon that rustling job we just finished in the Panhandle will be our last,' he went on. 'We weren't far off being caught then, and we had to leave behind half the cattle we'd collected.'

He got up, and beckoning Barrett to accompany him, he walked out of earshot of the others, and stopped.

'Judging by your face, Clem, you ain't too happy about those two joining us,' he said.

'I figured,' said Barrett, 'that we didn't

need no help. And two more men on the job is going to cut down our share considerable.'

'There's plenty for everybody,' said Duggan. 'And don't forget, Hays is a big town. A couple more guns gives us a better chance of getting away after the raid. So that's how it's going to be.'

Barrett grunted, and the two men walked back to the others.

The following morning, Duggan and four of his men saddled up early. Duggan spoke to Jack and Dale.

'We're riding over to Forsett,' he said. 'Ten miles south. There's a store there, and not much else. We'll bring provisions back. We're running low. Dave here'll keep you company till we get back.'

When they had cleared up after the meal, Jack and Dale sat down with Taylor, and chatted. Taylor, who had never been into Missouri, was eager to hear more about the State, and their activities there. Calling on their imaginations, both Dale and Jack obliged with stories of bank and stage hold-ups. Jack seized on a temporary lull in the conversation, to express an interest in Taylor's activities.

'That last job of yours,' he asked. 'In

Kansas, was it?'

'No,' replied Taylor. 'It was on the Texas Panhandle – on the big JW spread there. We were doing pretty well, until the rancher got wind of us, and came after us with his men.'

He paused, and pointed to the horses on the picket line.

'Why don't you untie your horses, and let them graze on that stretch of grass over there, with mine?' he said.

'Good idea,' said Jack, and he and Dale did as Taylor had suggested, then returned to sit with him.

'Good horse you've got there,' Taylor said to Jack.

'You're right,' said Jack. 'A good, strong horse. I took it from a homesteader in Missouri. Left him my own, which weren't half as good. That homesteader weren't too pleased, I can tell you.'

'The same sort of thing happened with Duggan,' said Taylor. 'You saw that big white of his?'

'Couldn't miss that,' replied Jack. 'A fine animal.'

'Well,' said Taylor. 'When we were on that rustling operation in the Panhandle I was telling you about, we were holding a small herd of JW cattle in a valley right on the

89

north boundary of the JW range. One day, this man who said he was a rancher from Colorado called Kilgour, rode in fast, on that same white horse we've just been talking about. There were four Comanches right behind him. We killed off the Indians, but soon after, we saw a bunch of JW ranch-hands a long ways off, heading our way. There were too many to fight off.'

'So you had to leave?' said Jack.

'That's right,' said Taylor. 'We headed fast up the valley, and were well out of sight before the JW men got there.'

'What about the rancher Kilgour?' asked Jack.

'I was coming to that,' replied Taylor. 'I've got to hand it to the boss. He thought pretty quick, and creased Kilgour with a shot along the side of his head, so's the JW men would think the Indians had hit him. Then we rode out with the papers the rancher had been carrying. The boss took a fancy to the white, and left his own horse behind. We rode along to another place, where Mort was holding another small herd we'd collected, and drove them into The Indian Territory, and sold them to a drover there.'

'Was the rancher hurt bad?' asked Jack.

'No,' replied Taylor. 'It was just a graze. I

reckon it wouldn't have taken long before he came round. We had a few laughs about it afterwards. There he was, alone with some stolen cattle and a running iron, and with no identification on him. And heading straight for him was this bunch of JW riders. We wondered just how he'd talk his way out of it.'

'Yes, I can see how the funny side of it would strike you,' said Jack, suppressing with great difficulty the intense anger which was boiling up inside him.

Shortly after, Taylor left them for a while, and Jack and Dale had a chance to talk together.

'I can see the news of your father ain't good,' said Dale. 'Can you figure out what's happened to him?'

'No, I can't,' replied Jack. 'Weaver of the JW told me he'd been having trouble with rustlers, but he said he'd seen no sign of my father.'

'What do we do now?' asked Dale.

'First, we have to make sure Duggan and his gang are all taken by the law,' replied Jack. 'Then I'm riding back to the JW, to find out what happened to my father.'

# SEVEN

Duggan and his four men returned in the middle of the afternoon, and four days later, they all left the ravine early, and headed north for Hays. They travelled slowly, avoiding any large settlements, and two days after leaving the ravine, they stopped around noon, at a point, just off the trail, a few miles south of Hays. Duggan spoke to Jack and Dale.

'You two ride into town,' he said, 'and have a good look at the bank, outside and in. I want to know when it opens and closes, and how many people work there. We know there's a vault inside, but I want to know where the key's kept. And it goes without saying that you ain't got to act suspicious.'

'You can count on us,' said Jack.

'At five o'clock this afternoon,' said Duggan, 'Clem will be waiting here for you, to bring you along to the hide-out.'

After parting from Jack and Dale, Duggan and the others rode east for a mile, away from the main trail, and approached a lone homestead, bordering a small stream. A man came out of the small timber house as they rode up to it, and stopped in front of him. He was a homesteader, distantly related to Duggan, Ford by name.

'Been expecting you, Vic,' he said to Duggan. 'The job's on, then?'

'Yes,' replied Duggan. 'We do it tomorrow. We'll stay here till then. But there's something I want you to do for me right away.'

Duggan explained what he wanted, and Ford quickly saddled a horse, and rode off.

When Jack and Dale rode into Hays, they stopped outside a restaurant opposite the Town Marshal's Office, and had a quick meal. Then they walked over to the Marshal's Office, and stood outside it for a short time, reading the wanted posters on the wall. None of them related to the Duggan gang, but Jack noticed a large one offering a big reward for a gang of bank robbers led by a man called Deacon, who had been operating in West Kansas.

Jack looked up and down the street. There was only one man in sight, a stranger to Jack, standing by his horse, outside the saloon.

Jack and Dale went into the Marshal's Office, where they found Marshal Bailey seated at his desk. Jack liked the look of him. He was a lean, middle-aged man, about five eight, clean-shaven, and with a dependable look about him.

The marshal leaned back in his chair. 'What can I do for you?' he asked.

'I came in to see if you have any wanted posters on a gang of outlaws led by a man called Duggan,' said Jack. 'I'm pretty sure I can tell you where they are.'

Marshal Bailey sat up in his chair.

'If you can do that,' he said, 'there's a lot of folks in Kansas going to thank you for it. The law's been after them outlaws longer than I like to remember. And I reckon they must have killed at least five innocent people by now.'

He rummaged in a drawer for a while, then handed over several wanted notices. Jack and Dale looked them over. They contained pictures and descriptions of all the present members of Duggan's gang, except the latest recruit, Manton.

'These men,' said Jack, handing the poster back to the marshal, 'are all a few miles from here. And there's a new man with them called Manton. That makes six in all.'

Jack went on to tell the marshal the full story of his father's disappearance, and how he and Dale had joined up with Duggan and his gang. He also told him why Duggan had sent them into town, and exactly where they were to meet Barrett later that day.

Just as he finished speaking, the door opened, and a big man wearing a deputy marshal's badge walked in. He was wearing a gun on his right hip, and a Bowie knife on his belt. His face was burnt deep brown, and his long black hair fell down to his shoulders. Jack estimated his age as being in the mid-fifties.

'This is one of my deputies, Zeke Hardy,' said Bailey, and proceeded to repeat to Hardy all that Jack had just told him. Hardy's eyes lit up.

'That's good news,' he said. 'Duggan killed a good friend of mine. I've been wanting to catch up with him for a long time.'

The marshal thought deeply for a while. Then he spoke.

'I'm going to bring the county sheriff in on this,' he said. 'That's Sheriff Lawton. We'll work together, and I reckon this is the way we should play it. When you two leave town later on, to meet up with Barrett, Zeke here will follow you to the place where Duggan is hiding out.'

Jack cut in. 'That could be dangerous for

Zeke, if he's spotted,' he said.

The marshal smiled.

'I can see you ain't heard of Zeke before,' he said. 'Zeke was an army scout for a long spell, and there's many a soldier owes him his life. If Zeke follows you and Barrett, and he don't want to be seen, he *won't* be seen. I can guarantee that.

'As I was saying,' he went on, 'Zeke will follow you, and at the same time, he'll leave a clear trail for me and Lawton and the posse to follow. We'll set off just before dusk, and meet up with Zeke near the hideout. Lucky it won't be too dark tonight. Moon's pretty near full.

'We'll surround the hide-out, wherever it is,' he went on, 'and hit it after midnight, when Duggan and his men are asleep. You two stay awake, and as soon as you hear me shout out, make a break for cover, and join us. Then we'll take the others.'

'Right,' said Jack. 'Of course, we don't know if we'll be sleeping in a building, or outside in the open. But if we're outside, we'll bed down near cover if we can, well away from the rest.'

'I want to do it this way,' said the marshal, 'because if we set up an ambush for them in town, when they come to rob the bank, there's always the risk that some innocent citizens might get shot.'

'Right,' said Jack. 'That makes good sense. We'll be leaving around half past four this afternoon, then.'

Hardy nodded. 'I'll be right behind you,' he said. Jack paused before leaving the Marshal's Office. He spoke to Bailey.

'If you want to check up on my story,' he said, 'you can contact Sheriff Colby in Pueblo, Colorado. He knows a lot of what I've just told you.'

The marshal looked at Jack.

'I don't figure there's any need for that,' he said. Jack and Dale left the Marshal's Office, and went through the motions of taking a surreptitious look at the bank premises from the outside. Then Jack went inside, and asked for change for a banknote. He could see that the staff consisted of one cashier, and an elderly man, the bank president, who sat at a desk behind the cashier. Behind the president, Jack could see the vault, and as he watched, the man at the desk got up, took a key from his pocket, and opened it.

Jack checked the opening and closing times on a notice on the wall, and felt he now had sufficient information to satisfy

Duggan when they saw him later on.

At half past four, Jack and Dale rode out of town, heading south. As they passed the Marshal's Office, they saw Hardy standing outside.

Barrett was waiting at the place where they had parted company the day before, and they followed him to the Ford homestead. From time to time, Barrett looked back along the trail they had just traversed. They tried to draw him into conversation on the way, but it seemed like he just wasn't in the mood for talking.

Duggan and the others were standing outside the house with Ford, when they arrived. As Jack and Dale dismounted, and turned to face Duggan, they found themselves covered by three guns, including Duggan's.

'Tie them hand and foot,' said Duggan, 'and sit them against the house.'

When this had been done, the gang leader walked up, and stood looking down at the two bound men. His face was convulsed with anger.

'I had you two watched in town,' he said, 'and I'd sure like to know just who you are, and what you said when you were having that long talk with the marshal and his deputy. Could be you're lawmen, and that's something I aim to find out.'

Jack thought fast.

'Lawmen!' he said. 'You've seen that wanted poster. Sure, we spoke to the marshal and his deputy, but it's easy to explain. I had an idea, riding into town, about how we might make things easier for ourselves when we hit the bank. So we went to the marshal's office, and had a good look at the wanted posters outside.

'There was one there,' he went on, 'offering rewards for the Deacon gang. So we had a good look at their pictures, and the information on the poster, then we went inside, and told the marshal we'd seen Deacon and his men yesterday, camped out in a ravine about thirty miles north of here. We said we were sure it was them, because we'd watched them from cover for a while. And we told the marshal it looked like they'd settled in there for a spell.'

Duggan looked at Ford.

'They *did* look at those wanted posters for a while,' said Ford.

'Go on,' said Duggan, to Jack.

'The marshal got a mite excited at the idea of getting his hands on the Deacon gang,' said Jack, 'and he said he was going to join up with Sheriff Lawton, and take a posse north to that ravine we told him about, at first light tomorrow.

'You can see what that means,' continued Jack. 'When we ride into Hays tomorrow, there'll be no lawmen there to get in the way.'

Duggan, still scowling, slowly lowered and holstered his gun. His men did likewise.

'Let me tell you right now, Kincaid,' said Duggan. 'There's only one man does the thinking for this outfit. And that's me. You do anything like that again, and you'll be sorry.'

Looking suitably chastened, Jack went on to tell Duggan all he had learned about the bank.

'Right,' said Duggan. We'll hit it in the morning then, after that posse has left. And after we've done the job, we'll head down south, into The Indian Territory, and lay low there for a while.'

Ford got some supper ready, and after they had eaten, the men chatted for a while. Then, one by one, they lay down for the night. Ford went to his bed inside the house. Jack and Dale lay down a little way from the others, and close to a small thicket and the picket line to which the horses were tied.

It was about half an hour after midnight when Jack heard someone shout his name. He and Dale rose immediately, ran to the picket line, slashed it, and chased the horses off. Then they ran into the thicket, before Duggan and the others were fully awake. Hardy met them there, and took them to Marshal Bailey.

'How many are there?' Bailey asked Jack.

'Seven,' replied Jack. 'That's counting a homesteader called Ford.'

The marshal, and the sheriff beside him, fired their rifles in the air, and at the pre-arranged signal, the members of the posse surrounding the outlaws fired off a few shots. There was a burst of return fire from Duggan and his men, but there was nothing for them to aim at, and it soon died down.

From cover, the marshal shouted to the outlaw leader.

'This is Marshal Bailey, Duggan,' he called. 'We've got you surrounded. You don't stand a chance. You might as well surrender now.'

'You go to hell,' shouted Duggan, and he and his men fired off some more blind shots, then retreated into the cover of the house. The posse pinned them in there until the following noon, when, after a fusillade of rifle fire from the posse, directed at the house, the outlaws finally surrendered, and threw out their guns.

Duggan was the first to walk out of the house, with his arms raised. He cursed, as he saw Jack and Dale standing with the posse.

'So you're lawmen after all,' he said. 'I should have finished you off when you got back from town.'

'We're not lawmen,' said Jack. 'My name's Kilgour. It was my father you knocked out, and left with that rustled herd in that valley in the Panhandle. And you stole his horse. Don't suppose you feel like telling me just where that valley is, do you, Duggan?'

'Go to hell,' replied Duggan.

'You deserve everything you get from the law,' said Jack, and watched, as the posse led Duggan and the others away. He and Dale followed on behind.

The following morning, in Hays, Jack sent a telegram to Jim Morgan on the Diamond K, asking if there was any news of his father. The reply from Jim, received the following day, said that there was no news of Joe Kilgour, and that all was going well on the ranch.

Dale also sent a telegram to his parents in

Kansas City, Missouri, asking how they were faring. His father ran a small general store there. He came into Jack's room at the hotel, in the early evening, with the answer in his hands.

'News from home ain't so good,' he said. 'My father's been took ill. He's in bed. Been there a few weeks. I've got to go and help out.'

'I'm sorry,' he went on. 'I was figuring to ride to the Panhandle with you, to help find out what happened to your father.'

'I'm sorry you can't come,' said Jack. 'I'm sure beholden to you for helping me hand Duggan and his men over to the law.'

'Can't say I did much,' said Dale.

'You were there, weren't you?' asked Jack. 'And I knew all the time, that if the whole thing blew up, there was somebody there to give me a hand. You leaving soon?'

'First thing tomorrow,' replied Dale.

'Same here,' said Jack. 'I'll head straight for the Panhandle.'

# EIGHT

After taking his leave of Dale, and the marshal and his deputy, Jack headed for the Lazy B, on the Panhandle. He was riding the big white gelding which had belonged to his father. Five days later, as he rode up to the ranch-house, he waved to Jasper, the foreman, who was standing near the corral. Mary Burley opened the door to his knock. Her eyes widened as she saw him, and she smiled.

'I promised I'd come back,' said Jack.

'I'm glad you did,' she said. 'Come in, and see father.'

She led him into the living-room, where her father was seated, and she and Jack sat down with the rancher.

Jack told them all that had transpired since he last saw them.

'I've come back,' he went on, 'to find that valley on the JW range where my father was left by Duggan and his gang. All I know is, it's somewhere on Weaver's north boundary.'

'You going to see Weaver first?' asked Burley.

'No,' replied Jack, 'I'm sure now that Weaver knows what happened to my father, and he sure won't tell me himself. I'm going to ride along that north boundary, and have a good look at every valley I come across.'

'It's a long boundary,' said Burley. 'Weaver's spread's a lot bigger'n mine.'

'I can't think of anything else to do,' said Jack. 'I've had a bad feeling for quite a while now about what's happened to my father. I think he might have died in that valley, but I'm pretty sure he was alive when the rustlers left him. I've got to find out what happened to him after they'd gone.'

'Your ranch in Colorado,' asked Mary. 'Is everything all right there?'

'Everything's fine there,' replied Jack. 'I left a good man in charge. I ain't got no worries on that score.'

'You want to be careful when you're nosing around on the JW range,' said Burley. 'Like I told you, Weaver's an unscrupulous man. If you need any help at all, come here. We ain't forgot what you did for Mary.'

Jack thanked him, then went on to question him about Weaver.

'When I was at Weaver's ranch-house,' he

105

said, 'I saw his daughter. But there weren't no sign of her mother.'

'She left him,' said Burley, 'about a year ago. Don't know where she is now. There were rumours that Weaver beat her. But there ain't no doubt that he idolizes the girl.

'If you do find out what's happened to your father,' he went on, 'you be sure to come back here, and let us know. Maybe we'll be able to help out in some way, if you find you're up against Weaver.'

Jack thanked the rancher again, and accepted his invitation to stay the night.

Jack left the next morning. Mary walked over to him as he was saddling up the white. She looked concerned.

'You be careful,' she said. 'Weaver's a bad man to cross, and he's got a big outfit. Are we going to see you here again?'

'Mary,' he said. 'When this is all over, you're going to see a whole lot more of me, if that's what you want.'

She looked him straight in the eye, and smiled.

'That's what I want,' she said.

Jack rode north across the Lazy B range, then across the JW range, to the east end of its northern boundary, giving the JW ranch buildings a wide berth. He saw no riders on the way.

After camping out for the night, he started riding west along the boundary, which, Burley had told him, followed a long ridge of high ground running east to west. He carefully examined every ravine or valley on, or close to, his path.

Just before noon, he saw in the distance what looked like the body of a horse, lying on the ground. As he rode up to it, he could see that there was a man lying on the far side of the horse, with the lower part of his body pinned underneath the animal. Jack quickly dismounted, and walked up to him, gun in hand. He took the man's gun from its holster. All the rounds had been fired, probably, thought Jack, in a vain attempt to call help. He put the gun back in the holster.

The man's eyes were open. He was groaning, and there was a trickle of blood from the corner of his mouth. He looked up at Jack.

'I'm done for,' he said weakly. 'Busted up inside. Darned horse stumbled for some reason, and fell, and rolled over on me before I could get my foot out of the stirrup.'

Jack had a look at the horse. Its foreleg was broken in two places.

'This horse is done for,' he said. 'I'll have to finish it off.'

Standing by the man on the ground, he held his Peacemaker against the horse's head, and fired. The horse's body jerked slightly, then became motionless.

'I'll drag that horse off you,' said Jack, walking towards his horse, to get the lariat hanging from his pommel.

'No!' screamed the man. 'Leave me be! Like I said, I'm all busted up inside. I reckon I ain't got long. Just leave me be.'

He coughed, and some blood gushed from his mouth.

Jack paused for a moment, then walked to his horse to get his water bottle. He took it over to the man, and gave him a drink, then squatted down beside him. As he did so, he spotted the JW brand on the side of the horse.

'Anything I can do for you?' he asked.

Weakly, the man shook his head.

'You a JW hand?' asked Jack.

The man nodded. 'Hank Randle,' he said. 'Been chasing strays out here.'

'Then maybe there's something you can do for me, if you've a mind to,' said Jack.

Surprised, Randle looked up at Jack. A spasm of severe pain distorted his face.

'I'm looking for my father, Joe Kilgour,' said Jack. 'He's a rancher from Colorado. Went missing around here a while back. Tall man, bearded, with grey hair, riding that white horse over there.'

Jack pointed to his horse.

'I know he was riding across JW range,' he said. 'Maybe you've seen him?'

Randle stared up at Jack, then lowered his eyes, and groaned again.

'I ain't had a good night's sleep since it happened,' he said, haltingly. 'Your father's dead. Hanged by Weaver's orders. We found him lying unconscious, near some rustled cattle. There was nobody else there, except some dead Indians. Your father told Weaver who he was, and how he happened to be in the valley with the cattle. And he asked Weaver to contact the sheriff in Pueblo. But Weaver took no notice, and he had your father strung up almost right away.'

'Where's the body?' asked Jack.

Randle closed his eyes for a few moments. Then he opened them, and spoke, more slowly than before.

'Go ten miles west of here,' he said, 'and you'll come to a long valley with a narrow entrance, and three cottonwoods standing together, about three hundred yards back from the entrance. Your father is buried under the first one you come to, riding up the valley.'

Randle's eyes closed, and he appeared to lose consciousness for a moment. Then his eyes opened again.

'Who was there when my father died?' asked Jack.

'I was there,' replied Randle slowly, pausing now and then for breath, 'and Weaver, and Stringer, his foreman. And there were two gunfighters called Sully and Quaid, who'd been taken on by Weaver when he was having trouble with homesteaders. I figured them for a couple of killers, who'd do anything for money. They left the JW soon after the hanging. From something I overheard, I think they were heading for South Texas.'

Exhausted, Randle closed his eyes. Jack waited until he had recovered a little, then spoke to him again.

'If I write out a statement with those names in it, will you sign it?' asked Jack.

'It was wrong to lynch him,' said Randle. 'Weaver should have checked his story. I tried to stop it, but it weren't no good. The others took no notice of me. They all agreed that he should die.'

He closed his eyes again.

'Would you sign a statement?' asked Jack again.

Randle's eyes slowly opened. 'Yes,' he said. 'They did wrong. But you'd better make it fast.'

Jack took some paper and a pencil from his saddlebag, picked up a flat stone to lay the paper on, then wrote on the paper:

'Joe Kilgour of the Diamond K was hanged by five men. Jason Weaver, Walt Stringer, Sully and Quaid and myself.'

'It's ready to sign,' said Jack, holding the paper in front of Randle's eyes. Randle slowly read the statement, then held his hand out, took the pencil, and signed the paper. His hand shook slightly, but the signature was quite legible. Five minutes later, as Jack sat by his side, there was another haemorrhage, more severe this time, and he died.

Jack left Randle where he was. He was sure that someone would come looking for the ranch-hand before long. He removed all traces of his own presence there, then rode westward, with the ridge of high ground on his right, and eventually came to the valley which Randle had described. He rode into it, and stopped at the first cottonwood he came to. He dismounted, and walked slowly round the tree several times. Finally, he stopped at a place where the ground appeared to have been disturbed.

He hunted among the stones lying on the valley floor, until he found a long, thin, flat piece, suitable for digging. Going back to the tree, he started digging, using the stone to loosen the soil, then scooping the soil up with his hands, and throwing it aside. It was slow work.

He was down about a foot, when a small piece of coloured material showed up. He cleared the earth around it, to reveal a larger area of material. The pattern on the material was the same as that on the shirts which, as Jack knew, had been habitually worn by his father. Slowly, he removed more earth, to reveal the decomposing remains of a human body. He carried on until he was absolutely certain that the corpse was that of his father. Then he pulled from around the corpse, a leather belt with a distinctive buckle, which he had given his father as a present, some years ago. Badly shaken at the sight of the remains, he returned the loose earth into the grave.

When he had finished, he stood by the

grave for several minutes. Inside him arose a grim determination to bring to justice the four men responsible for the death of an innocent man.

He mounted his horse, and headed back towards the Lazy B, keeping a close watch for JW riders. Once he saw two in the distance, and hid until they were out of sight. On the Lazy B, Mary, looking out of the ranch-house window in mid-afternoon, saw him approaching. At the same time, her father rode in with his foreman, from the south.

Jack went into the house with Mary and her father, and told them about finding Randle, and later, the body of his father. He also told them the names of the three men who, when called on by Weaver, had agreed to the lynching of Joe Kilgour.

'Weaver is a hard man,' said Burley, 'but I never thought he'd go this far. What're you aiming to do now?'

'I'm going to ride to Amarillo,' replied Jack, 'and see the Ranger Captain there. I'll tell him what's happened here, and I'll ask him to have Weaver and the other three arrested.'

'You'll come back with the Rangers?' asked Mary.

'Yes,' replied Jack, 'I aim to see the job finished.'

'Does Weaver know that you've found the body?' asked Burley.

'I don't think so,' replied Jack. 'I didn't leave no sign behind. I figured to surprise Weaver when I got back with the law, so I'd be obliged if you'd keep what I've just told you to yourselves.'

'You can count on that,' said Burley.

The following morning, Jack took his leave of Mary and her father, and headed for Amarillo. He arrived there the following day, and after booking in at an hotel, he went to the Ranger Headquarters. He was taken to see Captain Bart Rossman, a rangy Texan in his fifties.

Jack told Rossman the whole story, including the arrest of the Duggan gang, and showed him Randle's statement, and his father's belt. Rossman listened attentively, and leaned back in his chair when Jack had finished.

'Looks like Weaver and his men are guilty as hell,' he said. 'What would you like me to do?'

'I want them arrested pronto,' replied Jack, 'and brought before a court. People like Weaver shouldn't be allowed to take the law into their own hands.'

'You're plumb right there,' said Rossman, 'but there's a problem. All my men are tied up just now, chasing cattle rustlers and Indians on the borders. And they're likely be tied up for quite a while.'

'Can you take me on as a ranger, and I'll do the job myself?' asked Jack.

'You think you're up to it?' asked Rossman.

'Well,' replied Jack. 'I did have a hand in delivering Duggan and his gang over to the law.'

Rossman thought for a moment before he replied.

'What I'm going to do,' he said, 'is get in touch with that Marshal Bailey in Hays, Kansas, that you talked about, and see if he confirms your story, I should get a message back from him tomorrow. You come in and see me tomorrow afternoon, and I'll let you know what I've decided.'

The following afternoon, Jack went back to see Rossman.

'I've just heard from Marshal Bailey,' the ranger told him. 'He reckons you did a durned good job helping to get Duggan and his men arrested. I'm going to enlist you in the Rangers for the purpose of bringing those four men to justice. But before I do this, I need to have your word that you'll do your best to bring them here to be tried, and that you'll only kill if there's no other option. I can guess how you feel about the men who hanged your father, but if you can't give me your word on this, I don't want you in the Rangers.'

'You have my word,' said Jack, and Rossman swore him in.

'I reckon you'd best go after Weaver and Stringer first,' said Rossman. 'At least you know where they are. But it ain't going to be easy. Weaver's got a lot of hands to back him up.'

He rummaged in his desk drawer, took out a sheet of paper, and consulted it. Then he spoke again.

'I've decided you need a partner,' he said. 'And I've got just the man for you. He was shot up about a month ago, and he's just about fit for duty again. He's a Seminole-Negro.'

'A Seminole-Negro?' said Jack. 'Can't say it's a combination I've heard of before.'

'I'm not surprised,' said Rossman. 'There ain't that many around. They come from runaway slaves, who joined up with the Florida Seminole tribe, which was forcibly moved west by the Government. A lot of them ended up in Mexico, and some of them came back to Texas, and joined the Army, as scouts. And we've got a couple in the Rangers. The one I'm putting with you is Joseph Marks.'

'Are they good fighting men?' asked Jack.

'Mostly they're used because they're the best scouts around,' replied Rossman. 'When it comes to following a faint trail, they're in a class of their own. And, if needs be, they can live off desert terrain a sight longer than any white man could.

'But Joseph Marks is more than just a good scout,' he went on. 'He's not what you'd call a real gunfighter, but as well as being a good tracker, he can handle a knife better'n most, and he's pretty handy with a rifle, if needs be.

'And when he was working for the Army,' Rossman continued, 'he got friendly with an Irish sergeant, who was an ex-prizefighter. The sergeant had a few rounds with Marks, and it turned out he was a natural fist-fighter, and it wasn't long before the sergeant himself was finding him too hard to handle. Come in first thing tomorrow, and you'll meet him. Then you can set off for the JW range.

'You'll be in charge of the operation,' he went on, 'but if you have any sense, you'll take heed of what Marks says, and you won't be slow asking his advice if you're in trouble.'

Jack met Marks the following morning at Ranger headquarters. He was a man a little below average height, dark-complexioned, stocky, and very broad across the shoulders. His features betrayed, only slightly, his negro ancestry. He looked Jack straight in the eye when Rossman introduced them.

Marks was plainly dressed, in pants and boots, and a tunic buttoned all the way down the front. He wore a Texas hat, a Colt .45 on his right hip, and a hunting knife in a sheath attached to his belt. He spoke good English.

Rossman briefed them.

'So far as we know,' he said, 'there are four men alive who were there when Joe Kilgour was hanged. I want those four. Looks like you'll be able to bring Weaver and Stringer in first, then you can go after the other two. Good luck.'

After Jack and Marks left Rossman's office, Jack noticed how lightly Marks moved on his feet, despite his weight.

'You ready to leave soon?' Jack asked him.

Marks nodded. 'Ready in thirty minutes,' he said. 'See you here.'

'We'll head for Weaver's ranch,' said Jack. 'It's likely we'll find Weaver and Stringer there. I've got a feeling it's not going to be so easy to find the other two.'

Marks nodded. 'We will find them all,' he said. 'This man Weaver,' he went on. 'The man who ordered the hanging of your father. He has many men?'

'I guess so,' said Jack. 'It's a big spread he runs. We'll have a lot better chance of taking him and Stringer in if we can separate them from most of the ranch-hands somehow. And I've got an idea about that. We can talk about it while we ride.'

# NINE

On the day following their departure from Amarillo, the two rangers cut across the Lazy B range, and rode onto the JW range. They continued north, giving the ranch buildings a wide berth. They saw plenty of grazing cattle, but no riders. Eventually, Jack turned east, and rode on for a few miles, with Marks by his side. He stopped at a spot on the range where the cattle had thinned out considerably, and where the range was well covered with grass, and numerous patches of thick brush.

'We'll stay here for the night,' said Jack. 'We can hide in that patch of brush over there.' He pointed to a thick patch of brush two hundred yards away. 'And in the morning we'll start a range fire here. I figure we're close enough to the JW ranch-house for Weaver and his men to see the smoke when the fire starts.

'And,' he went on, 'Weaver's bound to send as many men out here as he can spare, and if the wind stays like it is now, the fire won't get out of hand, but it should take them quite a while to put it out. If Weaver stays behind, there'll be plenty of time to get him away from the ranch, and well on the way to Amarillo, before his men put the fire out.

'So we'll just have to pray,' Jack continued, 'that Weaver doesn't ride out with his men.'

'What about Stringer?' asked Marks.

'Well,' replied Jack, 'if we're really lucky, he'll stay behind with Weaver, and we'll take them both.'

Marks grunted, and they rode over to the brush patch, and made camp for the night, keeping a close watch for approaching riders. Marks didn't talk a lot at first, but after they had taken supper, he opened up a little, in response to Jack's friendly attitude. He told Jack about his part in numerous Army campaigns to counter Indian raids along the Texas-Mexico frontier, and by the time they turned in, they were on first-name terms.

The following morning, about an hour after sunup, they started the fire, which soon began to move across the range, under the influence of a light breeze, generating billowing clouds of smoke. Quickly, leaving the fire behind them, they rode south-east, to a vantage point – a small grove of trees – not far from the JW ranch-house, from which Jack could watch through his field-glasses for the ranch-hands who would soon be heading for the fire.

It was not long before Jack spotted, through the glasses, a bunch of riders coming from the direction of the JW ranch-house, and moving fast towards the smoke cloud, clearly visible to the north. He counted eleven in all. Jack and Marks waited until the riders were out of sight, then they rode up to the ranch buildings.

Weaver and Stringer were standing just outside the ranch-house, looking towards the distant smoke. They turned as Jack and Marks approached, and looked intently towards the pair.

'We're in luck, Joseph,' said Jack to Marks. 'Those two are Weaver and Stringer. The shorter one is Weaver.'

They rode on, and stopped in front of the rancher and his foreman. Weaver recognized Jack.

'You still looking for your father, Kilgour?' he asked.

'Not any more,' said Jack. 'I found his body a week ago, buried in a valley on the northern boundary of your range. He'd been hanged. And I know that both you, and Stringer here, had a hand in the hanging.'

Weaver, then Stringer, made a move towards their guns, but they were too slow. Jack had them covered before their guns had left the holsters. They let go the gun handles, and raised their hands. Marks dismounted, took the guns of the rancher and his foreman from their holsters, and threw them well away, on to the ground. Jack dismounted, still keeping the two men in front of him covered.

Marks, with gun drawn, went into the bunkhouse, the barn, and then the cook-shack, from which he emerged with the cook, and stood him beside Weaver and Stringer. Then he went inside the house. He found Weaver's daughter Emily in the living-room, staring wide-eyed out of the window at her father, Stringer and the cook, standing there, their hands raised under the threat of Jack's Peacemaker. Marks searched the rest of the house. Then he went out, and walked up to Jack.

'There's nobody else around,' he said, 'except a young girl inside the house.'

He gestured towards a ranch-house window. Glancing at it, Jack could see the white, strained face of Emily through the glass. He turned his head to look at the rancher, as Weaver spoke.

'You'll be sorry for what you're doing, Kilgour,' said the rancher. 'You ain't got no right to come on to a man's property in this high-handed way. If you've got some crazy notion that I had anything to do with your father's death, you'd better let the law deal with it.'

'We *are* the law,' said Jack. 'We're both rangers, and we're taking the two of you to Amarillo for trial.'

'But you ain't got no proof that we had anything to do with that hanging,' said Stringer.

'I had a very interesting talk with one of your ranch-hands, Hank Randle, before he died on the north range,' said Jack. 'I got the whole story from him, and I got a signed statement from him as well. And that statement said that you two, as well as two men, Sully and Quaid, were present at the hanging.'

'You won't get away with this,' said Weaver. 'My men will be back here soon.'

'That fire we lit for them,' said Jack, 'is going to keep them busy for quite a while yet. And while they're working hard out there, we'll be heading for Amarillo. We'll

124

take your daughter with us, and leave her with Mary Burley of the Lazy B. She'll be safe there for the time being.'

He turned to Marks.

'Tie Weaver's and Stringer's hands in front of them, Joseph.' he said. 'We'll leave the cook here, but you'd better tie his hands and feet, so's he can't ride out, and warn the others. When you're done, you can watch them while I get three saddled horses ready. Sooner we get on our way, the better.'

Jack waited, near to the ranch-house, with his back to it, while Joseph went to his horse for some rope. Walking back with it, Joseph suddenly stopped dead in his tracks, staring at something behind his partner. Jack turned, to see that Emily had suddenly appeared in the doorway of the ranch-house, a wild, desperate look on her face. She was holding a Remington 10-gauge, double-barrelled shotgun, aimed in the general direction of the two rangers. The hammer on one barrel was cocked, and Emily's finger was on the trigger. The muzzles were wavering slightly, but Jack and Joseph both knew that if the trigger was pulled, they would be virtually cut in two. They stood motionless. Then they heard Weaver's voice.

'Emily,' he called. 'Keep the gun pointing

at those two. And pull the trigger if they move.'

Weaver and Stringer walked out of the line of fire of the shotgun, and picked up their six-guns, which Joseph had thrown down earlier. The cook followed them. Weaver spoke to the rangers, ordering them to throw down their guns. They both complied, and Stringer covered them, while Weaver walked over to his daughter, gently took the shotgun from her, and released the hammer.

'Well done, Emily,' he said. 'I'm proud of you. Everything's all right now. You go back inside, dear. I'll come in to see you soon.'

Emily went inside, and Weaver walked over to stand in front of the two rangers, with Stringer keeping them covered. The cook went into the cookshack.

'What do we do now, boss?' asked Stringer.

'It's clear what we have to do,' replied Weaver. 'We've got to get rid of these two rangers. Better tie them up, while we're thinking about it.'

Stringer picked up some rope, and tied Jack and Joseph hand and foot. Then, leaving them lying on the ground, he walked with Weaver out of earshot of the two rangers.

'I've just had an idea,' said Weaver. 'It's plain we can't let anybody know we've finished these two off ourselves, and we know there's been a party of Comanches roaming around these parts just lately. So we'll take them out on the south range, before the men get back, and make it look like they met up with a Comanche raiding party, and got themselves killed. I've got a Comanche war bow and some arrows in the house. We can shoot them both with a rifle, then fire a few arrows into them, and maybe lift their scalps as well, to make it look good.'

'But won't Ranger Headquarters just send somebody else after you?' asked Stringer.

'I've got some friends in high places in Amarillo, who owe me a few favours,' replied Weaver, 'and if we can pass the blame for the deaths of Kilgour and his partner on to the Comanches, I think there's a good chance I can fix it so that the Rangers won't bother us again.'

'What about the cook?' asked Stringer.

'I think I can make sure the cook don't say anything about these two rangers being here today,' replied Weaver. 'And when we get back, you can think up some excuse to send some men to work on the south range tomorrow, so's they'll come across the bodies.'

Weaver went into the cookshack for a talk with the cook, then he walked over to the ranch-house to see his daughter, while Stringer saddled two horses, and pushed rifles in the saddle holsters, and ammunition in the saddlebags. Weaver told Emily that he'd be away for a little while, and said she should stay in the cookshack with Clem Hart, the cook, until he got back. He knew she was fond of Clem, who had known her since she was a baby, and who idolized her.

While Weaver and Stringer were occupied, the two rangers had a chance to talk.

'Things ain't looking so good, Joseph,' said Jack, eyeing Stringer as he saddled the horses. 'I've got a feeling we're going out for a ride with those two, and only Weaver and Stringer'll be coming back.'

Jack's eyes widened, as he saw Weaver coming out of the ranch-house, carrying a Comanche bow, and a buckskin quiver holding half a dozen arrows. Jack's mind worked quickly.

'You see that, Joseph,' he said. 'You know what that means?'

Joseph grunted, and he nodded assent.

Stringer walked over to the two rangers, and while Weaver held a gun on them, he untied their hands and feet, and ordered them to mount their horses. Then Stringer and Weaver mounted, and with Jack and Joseph riding in front of them, they headed south.

About five miles from the JW ranch-house, the four men rode slowly into the mouth of a long, narrow gorge about half a mile long, with steep, high walls. Half way along the gorge, Jack could see Joseph looking intently at the top of the left-hand wall. Joseph turned his head, and spoke quietly to Jack.

'We've got company,' he said. 'Indians, I reckon. Better be ready for some action.'

A little way behind them, Weaver moved closer to Stringer, and spoke to him in a low voice, so as not to be heard by the two rangers.

'Just before we reach the end of the gorge,' he said, 'we'll pull our rifles out, and shoot those two rangers in the back. I'll take Kilgour. You take the other one. And shoot to kill.'

They had ridden on another twenty yards, when suddenly, ahead of them, at the end of the gorge, appeared a party of ten mounted Comanche Indians, in full war paint. They were whooping and yelling, heading straight for them, and picking up speed fast. Some carried rifles, others bows and arrows.

Already expecting trouble, the two rangers acted instantaneously, both wheeling their horses, and heading back along the gorge.

'Get Stringer's rifle,' yelled Jack to his partner, as he himself approached Weaver, who had been riding behind him, and was just starting to turn, having seen the approaching Indians. As Jack came up to the rancher, he pulled Weaver's rifle from the saddle holster, and headed along the gorge, towards a recess in the wall of the gorge, partially blocked by a large boulder. Joseph took Stringer's rifle in the same way, and followed Jack. Weaver and Stringer, now having wheeled their mounts, brought up the rear, to provide targets for the approaching Comanches.

Stringer was the first to be hit. A rifle bullet entered his back, and he fell from his horse. A second later, an arrow struck Weaver between the shoulder blades. He swayed in the saddle, then slumped forward, but did not lose his seat. He followed the rangers, as they rode into the recess. Jack took Weaver's gun from its holster. Then he and Joseph quickly dismounted, and turned to face the approaching Indians. Partially screened by the boulder, they opened fire with the Winchester .44 rifles they had taken from Weaver and Stringer.

Their fire was rapid and deadly. Before the leading Indians reached a point thirty yards from the place where the rangers were making their stand, five of them had gone down. The remaining five wheeled, and raced for the end of the gorge. One was half way there, when a bullet from Joseph's rifle struck him in the back, and he fell from his horse. The remaining four rode out of the gorge, wheeled, and disappeared from view.

As they did so, Weaver, who had been sitting, slumped forward on his horse, at the back of the recess, fell sideways from the saddle. As he hit the ground, the shaft of the arrow which protruded from his back snapped, and he yelled out in agony, then lost consciousness.

'Watch out for them Indians, Joseph,' shouted Jack, and ran over to look at Weaver. He turned him over to look at the arrow wound in his back, then laid him on his side. He went to the rancher's horse, and took the rifle ammunition from the saddlebag. Then he rejoined Joseph.

'Weaver's still alive, but I reckon he's done for,' he said. 'And Stringer as well,' he went on, looking along the gorge at the motionless figure of the JW foreman lying on the ground.

'You think those Comanches will come back, Joseph?' he asked.

'They will come back,' replied Joseph, 'but not until it is dark. They cannot get to us in daylight without being shot. And already they have lost six. They will wait until after dark. They are not fools. But you can be sure they are watching us now, to see if we leave this cover.'

'So we'll stay where we are,' said Jack, 'and be ready for them when they come after us later.'

'After dark,' said Joseph. 'I will go after them myself. They will not expect this.'

'I'll go with you,' said Jack.

'They will hear you,' said Joseph. 'I can work better alone. You can wait here, and fight off any Comanches who might come this way.'

They heard a strangled gasp coming from where Weaver was lying on the ground. Quickly, Jack walked over to the rancher, and looked down at him for a few moments. Then he walked back to Joseph.

'Weaver's dead,' he said. 'We'll take him and Stringer back to the ranch when we've got rid of these Comanches. Reckon all we can do now, is wait till dark.'

While keeping watch, they ate some food which was still in their saddlebags, and drank some water from their water containers. Then they settled down to wait.

The night, when it came, was quite dark. The sky was heavily overcast. Joseph prepared to leave, carrying a knife and a rifle.

'I figure those Comanches will be aiming to come after us in about an hour,' he said. 'So maybe I can surprise them first. I'll pick up Stringer's gun on the way. And when I come back, I'll call you. Don't want you shooting me by mistake.'

He turned, and melted into the darkness, and however much Jack strained his ears, he heard not the slightest sound of his partner's progress. He stood against the large boulder, straining his eyes in the darkness, watching for any movement in his vicinity. Twenty minutes had passed after Joseph's departure, when suddenly, from the direction of the top of the wall of the gorge, almost immediately above him, Jack heard a shrill scream, suddenly cut short, followed by the sound of a shower of small stones falling down the side of the gorge. Almost immediately after, came the sound of some heavier object sliding and bumping along in their wake.

Then, just within the limit of his vision, Jack saw a figure roll briefly along the bottom of the gorge, and come to a stop. The figure lay motionless. He waited for a moment, then ran over to it, his Peacemaker in his hand, and bent over it. He risked lighting a match, cupped in his hand, and breathed a sigh of relief. He was looking at a dead Comanche, with a stab wound in the neck.

Jack ran back to the boulder, and resumed his wait. A further fifteen minutes passed, then he heard a single rifle shot from near the end of the gorge, and shortly after the sound of this shot had died away, the stillness of the night was broken by the sound of running horses, then one further rifle shot. Then there was silence until a few minutes later, when Jack heard Joseph's call, and shouted to him to come in.

'Don't expect they'll bother us any more,' said Joseph. 'Only two got away, and one of them's carrying a rifle bullet. We can leave, come morning.'

When daylight came, they hoisted the bodies of Weaver and Stringer on to the back of Weaver's horse, and headed for the JW ranch buildings. About half a mile from the ranch-house, and out of sight of it, they tied Weaver's horse to a tree, and rode on to the ranch buildings. They stopped at the cookshack, and went inside. The cook was alone. He took a quick step backwards as he saw them, and dropped the plate he was holding.

'I didn't know for sure,' he said, 'but I had a feeling, when you left here yesterday, that I wouldn't be seeing you again.'

'That was the idea,' said Jack, 'but things didn't work out like Weaver planned. We ran into a Comanche war party, and Weaver and Stringer are dead. The Comanches killed them both. Their bodies are on Weaver's horse, tied to a tree half a mile south of here. We left them there, so's the girl wouldn't see them. You'll take care of them?'

The cook nodded.

'I reckon I'd better let the boss's lawyer in Amarillo know what's happened,' he said. 'Maybe he'll know where Emily's mother is.'

'I'm worried about the girl staying on here, with no women around.' said Jack. 'I've a mind to take her to Mary Burley on the Lazy B. She'd look after her till her mother could be located.'

'I think that's a good idea,' said the cook. 'I'm going to see her in the house right now, and tell her about her father. She's going to be mighty upset, but I reckon I'll be able to persuade her to come along with you. Wait right here.'

It was half an hour before the cook returned.

'She'll go with you,' he said. 'Seems like she met Mary Burley once, and they took a liking to one another.'

'Right,' said Jack. 'We'll leave in the morning. Now, before you do anything else, could you tell me something about two hands Sully and Quaid, who left a while ago?'

'A dangerous pair,' said Hart. 'I could never understand the boss taking them on.'

'Do you know where they were going when they left here?' asked Jack.

'I overheard them talking at supper one day,' replied the cook. 'They were going to Jurado, that's a town in South-west Texas, not far north of the Mexican border, and the Rio Grande. The way I heard it, a man there called Farren had a job for them to do. Can't tell you anything more than that. They wanted by the law?'

'They are,' replied Jack, grimly. 'Could you give me a description of them?'

'Sure,' said the cook. 'They were both about the same build. Around five nine, I'd say, and stocky. And both about forty years old. Sully had sandy hair, and a beard the same colour, but Quaid only had a moustache, and he was bald, and limped a bit. Both of them wore two guns. That's about the best I can do.'

'Thanks,' said Jack. 'That'll be a big help.'

# TEN

The two rangers left early the following morning, with Emily. She was quiet, and had obviously been crying most of the night, but she made no protest as the cook helped her on to her horse.

They approached the Lazy B ranch-house just as the light was fading. Burley was standing just outside the house, with Jasper by his side, talking to a group of his hands. They, and the horses standing beside them, looked travel-stained and weary. Burley's face was lined with worry.

The rancher recognized Jack as he drew closer. He spoke to his men. 'Get some rest,' he said. 'We'll ride again first thing in the morning.' Then, as the group dispersed, he turned to Jack, looking curiously at Joseph and Emily.

'It's bad news, Kilgour,' he said. 'Mary's missing. Went for a ride this morning, and didn't come back. We've been scouring the range all day, but we ain't seen hide nor hair of her or her horse.'

'Maybe we can help,' said Jack. 'Since I saw you last, I've joined up with the Rangers.' He pointed to Joseph. 'This is my partner Joseph Marks.'

He went on to tell the rancher of the recent happenings on the JW ranch, and explained why they had brought Emily along.

'She's welcome,' said Burley. 'Until Mary comes back, I'll get Conchita to look after her. She's the wife of one my Mexican hands.'

Burley spoke to Emily for a short while, then took her to a small house about fifty yards away, knocked, and went inside with her. After a short while, he came back to the two rangers.

'I sure can do with your help,' he said. 'What d'you figure we should do tomorrow? When Mary left here, she was heading south.'

'Joseph here,' said Jack, 'is one of the best trackers in the territory. We'll head south just before sun-up, and he'll pick up your daughter's trail. Better leave a few men here to guard the place.'

The two rangers, with Burley, Jasper and four ranch-hands, were getting ready to leave, just before sun-up, when one of the

139

men, who had gone to the pasture for a horse, came running back with a sheet of paper in his hand. He gave it to Burley.

'Found this tacked on the pasture fence,' he said.

Burley read the message on the paper, then handed it to Jack. The ranger slowly read out the roughly-scrawled words:

'BURLEY. YOU MADE A BIG MISTAKE KILLING TWO OF MY MEN. WE HAVE YOUR DAUGHTER. SHE WON'T GET AWAY THIS TIME. IT'LL COST YOU TWENTY THOUSAND DOLLARS TO GET HER BACK. GO TO THE LAW, OR SEND A SEARCH PARTY OUT, AND SHE DIES. YOU'VE GOT THREE DAYS TO GET THE MONEY IN USED BANKNOTES. PUT IT IN A SACK, AND THREE DAYS FROM NOW, THAT'S THURSDAY, RIDE OUT ALONE, AND PUT IT UNDER THE FLOORBOARDS OF THAT OLD SHACK JUST OFF THE TRAIL, THREE MILES SOUTH OF THE RANCH-HOUSE, AT FOUR IN THE AFTERNOON. THEN RIDE BACK TO THE RANCH-HOUSE. YOUR DAUGHTER WILL BE FREED THE MORN-ING AFTER.'

Joseph left the group, and walked over to

the pasture.

Desperately, Burley looked at Jack.

'What do we do?' he asked.

'What we *don't* do,' replied Jack, 'is ride out now. They'll be watching for us.'

Burley told the hands that he was calling off the search, then he turned to Jasper.

'Ned,' he said. 'I want you to ride to Amarillo for the money. I'll give you a letter to the bank president. And you'd better set off right away.'

The rancher went inside to write the letter, and when he came out with it, Jasper was ready to leave.

Standing with Jack, the rancher watched his foreman ride off.

'Maybe we'll need the money,' said Jack, 'but there ain't no guarantee that when they get it, they'll free your daughter. So I'm going to ride out with Joseph tonight, to see if we can find her, and without them spotting us first.'

Burley looked at Jack doubtfully.

'I really think it's the right thing to do,' said Jack. 'We're dealing with men whose word don't mean a thing.'

Joseph, who had rejoined them, nodded in agreement.

'One rider brought the message,' he said,

'four or five hours ago. He rode in from the south, and rode back the same way.'

'All right,' said Burley.

'Is there anybody around who knows the country south of here really well?' asked Jack.

'John Rossiter,' replied Burley. 'He did a lot of prospecting around here before I took him on. I'll get him for you. He's probably in the cookshack.'

He returned with Rossiter, a short elderly man, a few minutes later, and introduced him to the two rangers.

'The men who've taken Miss Burley,' said Jack, 'are likely hiding her somewhere south of here, not too far away. And they'll be at a place where they've got a good long view, all round, of riders coming their way. You got any ideas where they might be?'

Rossiter thought hard for a few moments before he replied.

'There are two likely spots,' he said, 'both just south of our south boundary. One is a rocky gully, the other a small box canyon.'

He went on to describe the features and locations of the two places he had mentioned.

Jack thanked the old man, then turned to Burley.

'Joseph and me'll leave at nightfall,' he said, 'and if you haven't heard from us by Thursday noon, you'd better take the money along to that shack.'

The two rangers left just after dark, and rode first to the box canyon which Rossiter had described. It was a clear night, and eventually they reached a large rock outcrop which Rossiter had told them was near to the canyon entrance.

'Better I go on alone to check that canyon,' said Joseph, and Jack nodded. It was almost an hour before he reappeared.

'They are there,' he said. 'It must be them. They have posted a lookout on top of the canyon wall. Just one man. There is a hiding place for us, in a hollow near the canyon rim, back from the entrance, where we can wait until daylight.'

Leading the horses, they took a circuitous route, well clear of the canyon entrance, and walked down into the hollow which Joseph had mentioned.

They rested until the growing light in the eastern sky was strong enough to allow them to look down into the canyon. They climbed out of the hollow, and taking cover behind two large boulders, they looked down the canyon towards the entrance.

They could see a camp fire, with a man standing by it, and four blanket-covered figures lying on the ground not far from the fire. When the light had grown a little stronger, Jack looked through his field-glasses at the four recumbent figures, one by one. Coming to the last one, he stiffened. He could clearly see Mary's long auburn hair above the top of the blanket.

'She's there, Joseph,' he said, handing the glasses over.

Joseph took a look, and handed the glasses back.

'It is good,' he said. 'Now we must work out a plan to get her away from those men.'

Down below, the four men had breakfast, and one of them took food and drink to Mary. The lookout came in for breakfast, and was replaced by one of the others.

'I reckon, Joseph,' said Jack, 'that we can take care of this situation after dark. If you can sneak up on that lookout, and put him out of action before he warns the others, I figure the two of us can take care of the other four as well, before they can harm Mary.'

Down in the canyon, Cass Drummond, the leader of the gang which was holding Mary, walked over, and stood grinning down at her. He was a big burly man, unshaven, and with a slight cast in one eye.

'Glad to see you're eating,' he said. 'No point in starving yourself. If you behave, and your pa does exactly what we told him to do, you should be together again next Friday.'

Mary looked up at him, scorn in her eyes. She made no reply. Drummond grinned again, and walked away to join Tandy, one of his men.

'What are your plans for the girl?' asked Tandy.

'Until that money's in my hands,' replied Drummond. 'No harm comes to her. What we do with her afterwards, I ain't decided yet, but it ain't likely she'll ever see her father again.'

For the rest of the day, Jack and Joseph kept the gang under observation. They saw that the lookout was relieved every three hours, and that Mary was left alone, except when food was taken to her.

It was half an hour after midnight, and an hour and a half after the last change of lookout, when Jack and Joseph made their way silently along the top of the canyon wall, towards the place where the lookout was stationed. Joseph was carrying a coil of rope. They stopped when they saw the glow of light from the end of a burning cigarette.

'Wait here,' said Joseph. 'I will come back for you.'

After Joseph's departure, Jack stared fixedly at the varying glow of the cigarette. Then he saw a fresh one being lit, and a moment later, the glow swung in a small arc, then dropped down, out of sight. Five minutes later, Joseph called out quietly, and suddenly appeared at Jack's side.

'We can go in now,' he said. 'The lookout is gagged, and tied with rope.'

'Let's go,' said Jack, looking down into the canyon, where the fire was still burning.

'When we get close to that fire,' he said, 'we should be able to see where they're lying. I expect Mary'll be in the same place as before. We'll put the first two men we reach out of action for a minute or so, so's we can get the drop on the other two. I reckon a tap on the head with the barrels of our six-shooters should do the trick.'

Joseph grunted assent, and the two rangers climbed down the slope outside the canyon, and walked round to the canyon entrance, then crept up towards the five blanket-covered figures, just discernible in the dim light from the fire. Stopping for a moment, Jack indicated to Joseph which of the two sleeping men he himself was going to deal with. Mary, he was sure, was the figure farthest away from him, on the other side of the fire.

Crouching, and holding his six-gun, each ranger approached, and reached his first intended victim, at the same time. They both lifted the blanket, and struck the man underneath, on the side of his head. Both men were stunned, and the rangers took their guns, then ran over to the remaining two men, held a gun to their heads, and took their guns also.

Jack tied the hands of all four men, then ran over to Mary. He could see her, wakened by the activity close by, sitting up, with her blanket around her shoulders.

'It's Jack Kilgour, Mary,' he called. 'Come to take you home. You're safe now.'

Mary rose to her feet, scarcely able to believe what she was hearing. Then, as Jack reached her, she stood up, and ran into his arms, sobbing with relief. When she had recovered a little, he took her over to Joseph, who was guarding the four men.

'This is my partner, Joseph,' he said. 'We're both rangers. And without Joseph's help, you wouldn't be free.'

'Thank you, Joseph,' said Mary.

'My pleasure, miss,' he replied.

The two rangers set off for the Lazy B ranch-house with their five prisoners, as soon as it was light. On the way, Jack told Mary of the deaths of Weaver and Stringer, and of Emily's presence on the Lazy B. As they came within view of the ranch buildings, a group of riders left there, and headed fast in their direction. As they drew close, Jack could see that it was Burley and several hands. The rancher rode up to his daughter.

'You all right, Mary?' he asked.

'I'm all right, father,' she said.

They all headed for the ranch-house.

'These are all the men responsible?' asked Burley.

'Yes,' replied Jack. 'Have you a building I could fasten them in, until we take them into Amarillo for trial? I'm going to ask for a special wagon, a jail-wagon, to be sent for these men. I reckon that will be the safest way of getting them to Amarillo. I'll send a telegram today.'

'There's a good, strong shed over there,' said Burley, pointing. 'It's empty just now.'

Jack and Joseph put the prisoners in the shed which Burley had pointed out, leaving them bound hand and foot. It was a stout, timber structure, with a strong padlock securing the door.

'We can't take any chances,' said Jack to Burley. 'We've got to stand a 24-hour guard on this shed. Could you spare some of your men to help out?'

'Sure,' replied Burley. 'You work out a rota, and tell me just what you want.'

As Burley walked off to speak to some of the hands, Mary beckoned Jack from the house. He went over, leaving Joseph to guard the shed. She invited him inside.

'I called you in, Jack,' she said, 'because I haven't thanked you properly for saving me. I was really worried there, for a while.'

'No more worried than I was, Mary,' said Jack. 'I sure wouldn't like to live through anything like that again.'

She looked at him, gravely.

'I'm wondering,' she said. 'When you leave here, will we ever see you again? I have a feeling that you're the kind of man who doesn't stay anywhere long enough to put down any roots.'

'Mary,' said Jack. 'There's one thing I just have to do. With Joseph's help, I'm going to bring in the last two of the men who killed my father. There's a chance we'll find them in Jurado.

'But when we've brought them two in,' he went on, 'I'm going to leave the Rangers. You were right when you said I was a drifter, but that's because I had no real reason for settling anywhere. My father didn't need me to help him run the ranch, and nobody else was depending on me.

'But if you say the word now,' he continued, 'as soon as I leave the Rangers, I'm riding straight to the Lazy B, and I'm going to see what you think of the idea of riding up to Colorado with me, and helping me run that ranch I own up there.'

'Assuming you've got marriage in mind,' smiled Mary, 'you don't have to wait for my answer. I think it's a great idea. And I'm pretty sure I can get my father to see it the same way. He's been throwing out some pretty heavy hints lately that it's time I found a husband.'

When, in response to Jack's telegram, the jail-wagon finally arrived, Jack went to take his leave of Burley and Mary.

'Mary says we'll be seeing you back here sometime,' said Burley. 'You'll sure be welcome. I've been finding her a bit hard to handle lately.'

He evaded a playful blow from his daughter.

'I'd be mighty relieved if I could hand over the reins to somebody else,' he went on.

The two rangers escorted the jail-wagon to Amarillo, and handed the prisoners into custody. A week later, all five were sentenced to long terms of imprisonment.

# ELEVEN

The day after the trial ended, Jack and Joseph headed for Jurado, on the trail of Sully and Quaid. When they arrived there, their first call was at the County Sheriff's Office. Sheriff Lombard was inside. He was a tall, lanky man, in his late fifties, grey-haired, with a tired expression. Yawning prodigiously, he looked up at the two rangers as they came in.

Jack introduced himself and Joseph, and told the sheriff of the reason for their presence in Jurado. He described Sully and Quaid. When he had finished, Lombard creased his brow, and closed his eyes, as if in deep thought. He was seemingly making a great effort to dredge up some information which might help the rangers. Finally, just as Jack was getting the impression that the sheriff had fallen into a deep sleep, the law officer opened his eyes, and shook his head.

'Those names, Sully and Quaid, and Farren, wasn't it?' he said. 'Those names and descriptions don't mean a thing to me.

Sorry I can't help you. If they do happen to come into town, I'll hold them, and get word to Ranger Headquarters.'

His jaws stretched in a huge yawn again, as Jack and Joseph left.

'Looks like he can't help us,' said Jack, when they got outside. 'I reckon I'll have to do some asking around town myself. You take my horse along to the blacksmith next door, Joseph, and get it shod. Meantime, I noticed they've got two saloons in this street. I'll pay them both a visit, and see if the barkeeps remember seeing the men we're after.'

'I will go to the blacksmith,' said Joseph. 'My horse also needs new shoes. But first I will go in the store.'

At the first saloon which Jack visited, the barkeep professed to have no knowledge of the three men Jack was seeking, and Jack felt sure he was telling the truth. At the second one, whose clientele were mostly Mexican, the Mexican barkeep, a small man, hesitated, then shook his head, when asked about the three men.

'This is Ranger business,' said Jack. 'If you know anything about these men, tell me now.'

'I know nothing, senor,' said the barkeep,

and moved quickly along the bar to serve a customer.

As Jack left the saloon, he glanced along the street towards the blacksmith shop. He could see his own white horse, and Joseph's pinto, standing there, just outside the shop, and Joseph standing alone, facing a group of white men. A Mexican, wearing a blacksmith's apron, was standing to one side. Quickly, Jack walked towards Joseph, and reaching him, stood by his side. Joseph was concentrating his attention on the three men in front of him, and he did not turn his head. But he knew that his partner was at his side.

One of the men who had been speaking to Joseph, broke off as Jack arrived, and stared at the ranger. He was an ugly man, swarthy and broad-faced, around medium height, and muscular. His name was Rafferty. There was an air of menace about him. His two companions, Blair and Dormer, were around the same height as him, but not so stocky. Each of the three men wore a right-hand gun.

Rafferty spoke to Jack.

'I don't know who you are, mister, but I was just telling this man he'd have to wait till the blacksmith here tended to *our* horses.

I ain't seen anything like him before, but it's clear he ain't a white man. I've got a mind to run him out of town.'

'You were here first, Joseph?' asked Jack.

'I was here first,' replied Joseph.

'It don't make no difference who was here first,' said Rafferty. 'We don't aim to hang around waiting, while the blacksmith tends to the likes of him.'

'You ain't got no choice,' said Jack. 'You'll just have to wait till me and my partner's been attended to. And another thing, you'd better button your big fat mouth before you gets hurt.'

Rafferty's face purpled with rage, and his hand hovered near the handle of his six-gun. Blair and Dormer adopted the same posture.

'You just signed your own death warrant, stranger,' snarled Rafferty. Then he glared at Joseph. 'And yours as well,' he added. 'You know what to do, boys.'

The three mens' right hands moved the short distance to their gun handles, their fingers closed around them, and they started to pull the six-guns out of their holsters, Rafferty fractionally ahead of the others.

Then they froze.

Before any of the three guns had cleared leather, a bullet from Jack's Peacemaker had passed midway between the heads of Rafferty and Blair. As they stood motionless, and before they could continue their draws, Jack recocked his gun, and they found themselves looking down the barrel of his Colt. They were also covered by Joseph, who had drawn his own gun. They raised their hands, shoulder-high.

'Get their guns, Joseph,' said Jack, 'and drop them behind me.'

Joseph complied, then stood beside Jack, facing Rafferty and his partners.

'That man there,' said Jack, pointing to Rafferty. 'He said some pretty insulting things about you, Joseph. I figure you might like to teach him a lesson in manners.'

Joseph turned his head to look at Jack. His face, as usual, was pretty inscrutable, but Jack thought he caught a glimmer of gratitude and anticipation in his partner's eyes.

'I would like that,' said Joseph.

Jack spoke to Rafferty.

'I guess you know I could have killed you if I'd had a mind to,' he said, 'but it wouldn't have been fair to my partner here. He didn't take kindly to those things you said about him, and I know he wants to show that he's as good as a white man any day. You want to fight with knives or fists?'

'No knives,' said Rafferty. 'I want to get my hands on him.'

Joseph handed his knife to Jack.

'You two,' said Jack, speaking to Blair and Dormer. 'I've got my eye on you both. Try to take a hand in this, and you'll be sorry.'

Joseph and Rafferty moved out into the street a little way and stood facing one another. Joseph stood motionless, his dark face inscrutable, his arms by his sides, his massive shoulders hunched slightly forward. Rafferty, of similar stature to Joseph, but fatter around the waist, glared at the man facing him, his face displaying rage, and also anticipation. He was feeling supremely confident of the outcome of the fight. He was a quarrelsome man, with a history of hand-to-hand fights in the past, and he had never been beaten.

Impatient to get started, he quickly moved in on Joseph, raised his right fist, and aimed a blow, with all his weight behind it, at the side of the ranger's head. Joseph's feet didn't move, but the upper part of his body swayed backwards, then forwards again, after Rafferty's fist had passed in front of his face. While momentarily off balance, Rafferty was at the ranger's mercy, and Joseph caught him with two jolting, right-hand punches, one to

157

the ribs, and the other to the right ear.

Joseph stepped lightly backwards, and turned to watch his opponent, as he staggered sideways. Rafferty, incensed, recovered his balance, and shook his head. Then, cursing loudly, he rushed straight at Joseph, this time without telegraphing his intentions. His aim was to grab the ranger, and head-butt him. But when he reached for Joseph, the ranger wasn't there. At the last moment, he had sidestepped, and stuck out a leg in front of Rafferty, who lost his balance, stumbled forward, and ended up with his face ploughing through the dirt on the street. Slowly, he got to his feet, and faced Joseph again.

'Damn you, black man or Indian, whatever you are,' he said. 'Why don't you stay in one place, and fight it out like a real fighting man?'

He brushed the dirt off his face, spat some more out of his mouth, and walked up to Joseph, who obliged him by standing his ground. They traded punches for a while, and it was evident that the ranger's punches were doing a lot more damage than Rafferty's. The end came when, after a sudden flurry of punches, Joseph delivered a knockout punch to the side of Rafferty's jaw, and watched his opponent slump to the ground, unconscious. It was obvious that he was a beaten man.

'You feel better now, Joseph?' asked Jack.

'Better, much better,' replied Joseph.

Jack spoke to Blair and Dormer.

'I'm going to leave your guns with Sheriff Lombard,' he said. 'You can pick them up there later. I figure maybe he'll want to give you a lecture on how to behave when you're in Jurado.

'You'd better leave now,' he went on. 'The blacksmith's going to be busy for quite a spell. And take that man with you.'

He pointed to Rafferty, who was starting to stir. Blair and Dormer helped Rafferty to his feet, and leading their horses, they supported him as he staggered towards the nearest saloon. When they reached it, they disappeared inside.

The blacksmith walked up to Jack, smiling. He was a short man, with muscular arms.

'This white horse is yours, senor?' he asked.

Jack nodded.

The blacksmith stepped back a little, and looked the horse over.

'A fine horse, senor,' he said.

'A fine horse,' agreed Jack. 'Needs a new set of shoes.'

'Si, senor,' said the blacksmith. 'I will start on it right away. My name is Ramon.'

He looked over towards Joseph, who was examining the shoes on his own horse.

'Your friend, senor,' he observed. 'A real fighting man, that one. The man he has just beaten, the man Rafferty, is a bad man, senor. Many times he has spoken to me, Ramon, as if I am dirt. And many times, I have wished to show him I am no dog, to be spoken to like that.'

He shrugged his shoulders.

'But senor,' he went on. 'There are always three of them. And they are wearing guns. And I am alone.'

'I know, Ramon,' said Jack, 'that there are many white men who think they are better than the Indians, and the Mexicans, and the negroes. But I think that some day – it may take a long time – but some day, all law-abiding men will *really* be considered equal.'

'May that day come quickly, senor,' said Ramon, fervently.

'I hope you won't have trouble with Rafferty because of what happened here today,' said Jack, 'but if you do, just let me know. Me and my partner are both in the Texas

Rangers. We'll likely be staying here a few days.'

'I will let you know, senor,' said Ramon.

'You know some place where we can stay?' asked Jack, as they were leaving.

'Of course, senor,' replied Ramon. 'My sister Consuela has two rooms, and she can feed you. Good Mexican food. I will take you there now. It is not far.'

They walked with Ramon to the outskirts of town, to a medium-sized two-storey timber house, with a small garden at the side, where Ramon introduced them to his sister, and Consuela showed them two upstairs rooms. There was little furniture, but the rooms were clean, and the beds reasonably comfortable. As they came downstairs, a Mexican girl came into the house. She was about seventeen, judged Jack, and strikingly beautiful.

'This is my niece, Juanita,' said Ramon, proudly.

The girl smiled shyly, and went to stand by her mother.

'You will eat at seven, senores?' asked Consuela.

'Yes,' replied Jack. 'Seven will be fine.'

The rangers agreed with Ramon a time for them to pick up their horses. Then they

161

walked along the street to the Sheriff's Office. Lombard was still sitting at his desk, apparently half asleep. Jack told him of the trouble at the blacksmith shop, and laid the three guns on the desk. Languidly, the sheriff looked at them.

'I'm going to have a word with Rafferty about this,' he said. 'I'm going to tell him to stay out of town, if he can't behave reasonable. You rangers plan on staying long around here?'

'As long as it takes to find somebody around town who's seen or heard of those three men we're after,' replied Jack.

A flicker of annoyance passed across Lombard's face.

'I know everything that goes on in this town, Kilgour,' he said, 'and you can take it from me that those three ain't never been here. You're just wasting your time hanging around.'

'Maybe so,' said Jack, 'but we'll hang around a while longer anyway.'

Lombard grunted something, and settled back in his chair again. The two rangers left.

'That sheriff,' said Joseph, when they were outside. 'He is not a man we can trust.'

'I have the same feeling, Joseph,' said Jack. 'I don't think he likes having us around here.'

Joseph grunted agreement.

The two rangers walked back to the house of Ramon's sister, and rested in their rooms for a while. They had had a long ride that day. Then they went for their horses. Taking a look at Ramon's workmanship, they could see that he had done a good job. They paid him for the work.

'Senores,' he said, as they were about to leave. 'You are men of the law, and perhaps you can help. Consuela has no husband. He was killed by a drunken Americano, firing off his gun in the street. The sheriff said it was an accident, and he let the Americano leave town without punishment. It is well known by us that many people in Jurado think that the life of a Mexican is of no account.

'So, senores,' he went on, 'Consuela has been left without a husband, and Juanita without a father to protect her. And Consuela is much troubled because yesterday, and also seven days ago, three mounted Americanos have passed the house while Juanita was in the garden, the same three each time. Each time they have stopped, and talked to Juanita, but Juanita was frightened, and ran inside to her mother. The first time, the men stayed for a while, shouting for her to come out, then they rode on. But yesterday, senores, they stayed shouting for a long time before they left, and we fear that some harm may come to Juanita.'

'Do you know who those men are, Ramon?' asked Jack.

'No,' replied the blacksmith. 'They ride into town, and go into the saloon, and the store. They do not stay long. Then they ride out again. Nobody knows from where they come, and where they go.'

'So long as we are here, Ramon, we will watch out for Juanita as well as we can. She is a beautiful girl.'

'Muchas gracias, senores,' said Ramon, gratefully.

'Ramon,' said Jack. 'We are looking for three men called Farren, Sully and Quaid.' He described Sully and Quaid. 'We think they are in Jurado, or maybe they *were* here, and left. Do you know anything of these men?'

'No,' replied Ramon. 'But I have many friends. I will ask around.'

Jack pointed to the small saloon along the street.

'I had a feeling that the Mexican barkeep in there might know about the three men,' he said. 'But he wouldn't tell me anything.'

'I know him well, senor,' said Ramon. 'I will speak with him.'

Darkness was falling as the two rangers walked back to Consuela's house. They ate an excellent supper, complimented the smiling Consuela on the meal, and went out for a walk around the town. They returned about half an hour later, and were just about to enter the front door, when they heard a scream from behind the house. Jack ran around one side of the house, Joseph around the other. Jack paused as he reached the rear corner of the house, and peered round it.

The back door of the house was open, and the windows were uncovered. In the light spilling out from the house, Jack could see Consuela lying motionless on the ground, and two men struggling with Juanita, pulling her towards three horses which were standing in the background. A third man stood holding the horses.

Jack caught a brief glimpse of Joseph, moving just outside the lighted area, towards the man with the horses. He stayed where he was, so as to give Joseph time to neutralize this man, so that they could make a combined attack on the two men holding the girl. He saw the man go down, just as Juanita, screaming and sobbing, broke free, and tried to run into the house. The two men who had been holding Juanita cursed, and caught her again just before she reached the doorway.

Jack and Joseph approached the two men and the girl simultaneously, out of the gloom, and they moved so quickly, that the men had no time to react to their presence. Just as one of them was balling his fist to strike Juanita on the face, Jack laid the barrel of his Peacemaker along the back of the man's head, pulled the man's gun, and threw it away. At the same time, Joseph, approaching the other man from the rear, clamped his arm around the man's throat, and pulled tight. With his free hand, he pulled the man's gun, and threw it down. He maintained his tight hold around the man's neck until he lost consciousness. Then he let go, and the man slumped to the ground, and lay beside his partner. Then Joseph went over to the man who had been holding the horses, and dragged him along to lie beside the others.

Jack went over to Consuela. Juanita, still sobbing, followed him. Consuela had obviously been struck hard on the side of the face, but she was coming round. Jack helped her to her feet, and mother and daughter embraced for a while, until Juanita's sobbing ceased. Then Consuela released her daughter, and looked down at the three men who had attacked them.

'Pigs!' she said.

'Senora,' said Jack. 'As soon as these three can walk, we will take them to the jail. You would like a doctor to see your face?'

'No,' said Consuela, feeling it gently with her hand. 'Juanita will bathe it for me. We thank you, senores, for what you have done. But will not these men go free?'

'These men will *not* go free,' Jack assured her.

The three men on the ground were starting to stir as he spoke, and eventually all three, prodded on by the rangers, climbed to their feet.

'We're rangers,' Jack told them. 'We're going to hand you over to the sheriff.'

Shortly after, the three men walked unsteadily towards the Sheriffs Office, arms half-raised, with the guns of the two rangers at their backs.

The street was quiet, and they reached the Sheriffs Office without encountering anyone. It was in darkness.

Joseph stayed with the three men while Jack went in search of the sheriff. He walked along to the saloon next door, and went inside. He was about to ask the barkeep where the sheriff might be found, when he spotted Lombard, sitting at a table with another man, at the far end of the saloon. He walked over to him.

'We're holding three men outside your office, sheriff,' he said. 'Hope you've got room for them in your jail.'

Slowly, the sheriff rose to his feet.

'This was a reasonably quiet town till you came along, Kilgour,' he said. 'What's this latest trouble you've stirred up?'

Jack told Lombard exactly what had happened.

'You know as well as I do, sheriff,' he said, 'that these are serious offences. Assault on an innocent woman, and attempted kidnap of a young girl.'

The sheriff said nothing as they walked towards his office, but his face darkened. When he and Jack reached Joseph and the prisoners, they all went inside the office. Lombard lit the lamp, then peered closely into the face of each of the three prisoners in turn. Then he shook his head.

'Ain't seen any of these before,' he said.

'Like I told you, Sheriff, they've been in town twice before,' said Jack. 'Yesterday, and seven days ago. They only stayed a short

168

while each time. Visited a saloon and the store.'

'Could be,' said the sheriff. 'There's a lot of people coming in and out of town I don't see.

'I'm going to lock these three up,' he went on. 'Then, tomorrow, I'm going to telegraph the District Judge, and see where he wants them to be tried.'

'You got a deputy?' asked Jack.

'Not a permanent one,' replied Lombard.

'Right, then,' said Jack. 'These three are tough-looking hombres. And maybe they've got friends nearby, who might get the notion that it would be easy to bust in here, and set them free. So my partner and I'll take turns at guarding them here, day and night, until they go for trial.'

The sheriff hesitated for a moment, then he nodded.

'Be glad of your help,' he said, then took the prisoners through to the cells.

# TWELVE

Jack left Joseph at the jail, and walked back to Consuela's house. Ramon was there with her. One side of her face was badly swollen, and discoloured. The blow which had knocked her down had obviously been a severe one.

'Senora,' said Jack. 'Your face!'

'It is nothing,' said Consuela. 'Soon it will go.'

'And Juanita?' asked Jack.

'Poor child,' said Consuela. 'I have taken her to bed. But she is still very frightened. I think she will have bad dreams tonight.'

'My partner and I will be guarding the three men at the jail until they are taken for trial,' said Jack.

'This I am glad to hear,' said Consuela. 'The only place for such men is prison.'

'How long will you be guarding these men?' asked Ramon.

'It's hard to say,' replied Jack. 'Depends on the District Judge. Maybe a week, maybe more.'

When Jack went into the jail the following morning, to relieve Joseph, the sheriff told him he had just sent off the telegram about the prisoners. At around ten in the evening of the same day, Joseph came to the jail to relieve Jack, and they both sat talking for a few minutes in the Sheriff's Office, with Lombard, who said he was going to leave with Jack. As a knock sounded on the door, Lombard got up, and took a shotgun from a stand against the wall. He walked over to the door, and lifted a flap which allowed him to look through a small aperture in the door, at eye level.

'It's all right,' he said. 'Friends.'

Jack and Joseph relaxed.

Lombard unlocked the door, then turned to face the two rangers. The barrels of the shotgun were aimed halfway between them, and the hammer on one barrel was cocked. There was a murderous look on the sheriff's face.

Jack and Joseph knew better than to go for their handguns. They would both have been cut in two by the shotgun blast before they had triggered their Colts. They sat motionless, while two men entered the office, one limping slightly. Each of the men was carrying two guns, one of which he was holding in his hand.

Looking at the two men, Jack knew he had never met them before, yet something stirred at the back of his mind. Then he realized that they fitted the descriptions of Sully and Quaid.

One of the men relieved the two rangers of their guns. Then the other one spoke to Lombard, who was still holding the shotgun on Jack and Joseph.

'So these are the two lawmen looking for Sully and me,' he said.

'And these are the ones who brought Farren and the other two in last night.'

'These are the ones,' said Lombard. 'They're called Kilgour and Marks. It appears you hanged an innocent man up on the Panhandle, and the man you hanged was the father of Kilgour here.' He pointed to Jack. 'I guess he's sure itching to get his hands on you and Sully.'

Quaid and Sully stared at Jack. There was a look in his eye that, momentarily, sent a shiver through them. Then Sully looked away, and spoke to Lombard.

'Well, that ain't going to happen now,' he said.

'Till we heard from you this morning,' he went on, 'we couldn't figure out why Farren and the others didn't come back with that Mexican girl last night. We'd been looking forward to getting acquainted.'

'You'd better let Farren, and Scriven, and Platt, out of the cells,' said Lombard. 'I guess they ain't took too kindly to being locked up all this time, but I couldn't risk trying to free them till you got here. Key's on that hook on the wall.'

Sully took the key, and went through to the cells, returning shortly with Farren and the other two men, all looking somewhat the worse for wear. Jack guessed rightly that Farren was the tallest of the three, a man who looked like he was used to giving orders. He was obviously the leader of a gang consisting of himself and, at least, Sully, Quaid, Scriven and Platt. Jack wondered what particular brand of criminal activity they were engaged in.

Farren regarded the two rangers with a cold, calculating look. Then he turned to Lombard.

'We've got to get rid of these two, of course,' he said. 'But it's got to be done right. We don't want the whole place crawling with rangers. We've got to take them well away from here, and finish them off in some way that doesn't bring the law down on us. We can't risk botching it. I'm going to have to think pretty hard about what we do with them. Meantime, they can stay in the cells here, can't they, sheriff?'

'Sure,' said Lombard. 'Nobody'll know they're here. The man at the livery stable owes me a favour. I'll tell him to put the rangers' horses out of sight, and to say they rode off this evening in a hurry, if anybody asks. But I'll need a hand to keep guard on them till you take them away.'

'All right,' agreed Farren. 'Sully and Quaid can stay here.'

'You don't really think you can get away with this, do you, Farren?' asked Jack. 'Our Headquarters knows that we're looking for Sully and Quaid, and whatever you do to try and cover it up, they'll be sure those two had a hand in murdering us. And the Rangers don't give up easy.'

'I think I can work out a plan which'll throw them right off the scent,' said Farren, 'and you'll never know how successful it was. You'll both be dead.'

'If you're sure of that,' said Jack, 'maybe you'll tell us just what this gang of yours does, and how a crooked lawman like Lombard fits into the picture.'

Lombard moved towards Jack, with the

barrel of his Colt raised, but Farren waved him back.

'We've got to keep them in good condition for the time being, sheriff,' he explained. 'Until I decide exactly what we're going to do with them.'

He turned to Jack.

'No harm in you and your partner knowing what we're doing in these parts, Kilgour,' he said, 'since you won't be passing it on. We have an arrangement with the sheriff here that brings in a lot of money for all of us. The sheriff gets to hear of most of the movements of gold and currency inside his county. Him having a brother who works for the stagecoach line helps quite a lot.

'So every now and again,' he went on, 'we hold up a stagecoach, and help ourselves to the valuable merchandise we know it's carrying. And so that nobody gets too suspicious, we sometimes stop a stagecoach that's carrying nothing valuable, except maybe a few personal items belonging to the passengers.

'And after every hold-up,' he continued, 'the sheriff here rushes out, and painstakingly searches for the robbers in an area a long way from where he knows them to be.'

'A workable plan, for a while,' said Jack,

'but it depends entirely on the cooperation of a corrupt law officer, and I wonder how long it's going to be before people really start putting two and two together.'

'Maybe you're right,' said Farren, 'but I figure we can carry out a few more hold-ups yet, before we ride off with the profits.'

He turned to Quaid and Sully.

'Search these two,' he said. 'Make sure they have no weapons on them, then put them in that cell we were in.'

Quaid and Sully searched the rangers, then pushed them through the door leading from the office to the cells. This door was a strong one, fitted with a stout lock. There were two cells, one small one on the left, just inside the door, and a larger one, with two bunks, further back, at the rear of the building. The rangers were pushed into the larger cell, and the cell door was locked behind them. Quaid and Sully then went back into the office, locking the door behind them.

The rangers looked round the cell. There was a window high in one wall, the rear wall of the building. Under this window, one of the bunks was standing. Jack climbed on to it, and looked out of the window. The bottom sill was at shoulder level. It was dark outside, but Jack could just see that there was nothing between him and the open country outside town, except for one apparently derelict wooden building, just off to his left. He knew that the blacksmith shop was nearby, on his left, but it was out of his line of sight.

He looked at the vertical metal bars set in the window frame. They were stout bars, set close together, close enough to prevent a hand gun or rifle being passed through. Looking at the stonework into which the bars were set, Jack could see that it was soft stone, but he knew that without a suitable tool, it would be impossible to remove the bars. He stepped down off the bunk, and spoke to Joseph.

'Well, Joseph,' he said. 'Looks like we're in real trouble. You got any ideas?'

Joseph shook his head.

'Nothing we can do, so long as they're holding us in here,' he said. 'But maybe when they take us out, we can make a break for it.'

The rangers slept fitfully that night. During the following day, they saw only Sully, Quaid and Lombard. Food was brought to them three times during the day. On each occasion, the cell door was opened to pass the food tray in, and later, to take it out. The sheriff stood by with his shotgun.

At about an hour after midnight, the two

rangers were lying on their bunks. A small oil lamp had been left burning outside their cell door. Jack was wakened by a noise outside the cell window, followed by the impact of some objects dropping onto his bunk.

Quickly, he stepped up onto the bunk, and looked out of the window. He could just make out two figures, scurrying towards the derelict building. One was that of a man, short and broad, the other that of a young boy. They both disappeared behind the building.

Jack stepped down off the bunk, and examined, one by one, the three objects lying on the bed. The first was a small chisel, of the hardest steel. The second was a small hammer, with a metal head, and a wooden handle. The third was a hunting knife, with a strong, sharp, double-edged blade. Jack handed this to Joseph;

'I'm not sure,' said Jack, 'but I think it was Ramon who just brought these for us.'

He stepped onto the bunk again, with the chisel and hammer in his hand, and closely examined the bars, and the sill. Then he stepped down again, and sat on the bunk.

'We need to take about twelve bars out, Joseph,' he said. 'There's about an inch between the bottom of each bar, and the inside edge of the sill. So we'll have to cut twelve channels, from the bottoms of the bars to the inside edge of the sill. I reckon that when we've done that, we can pull the bars forward at the bottom, and they'll come free at the top.'

'Do we start now?' asked Joseph.

'Too risky,' replied Jack. 'They're liable to hear us, with everything quiet outside. We'll start after breakfast. That's a good chisel we've got. Maybe it won't take so long. We can lay something soft on the head of the chisel, to keep the noise down when the hammer hits it. And if I'm right in thinking that Ramon brought these things for us, I have a feeling he might be making a lot more noise than usual in his shop today.'

Later on, after the breakfast tray had been taken away, Jack stepped onto the bunk, and started work. Earlier, using the hunting knife, he had cut a small piece of leather from his boot, to hold on top of the chisel, to deaden the sound of the hammer blow. He worked steadily, watching carefully for anyone moving outside the window, while Joseph listened for the sound of the key turning in the lock of the door leading to the office. He pushed and blew out of the window, the loose stone and powder which

179

he had chiselled out.

After an hour, he changed places with Joseph, and they continued the work steadily, between them. Jack had noticed that there appeared to be greatly increased activity in the blacksmith shop, particularly on the anvil, compared with the previous day.

They were interrupted at midday, when a meal was brought in. The small channels on the sill which had already been cut, were above eye level, so there was little chance of them being noticed against the light coming in from outside.

They continued for a further hour after the meal tray had been taken away. Then Joseph heard the key in the door. Jack quickly stepped down from the bed, hid the tools, and sat down. Farren came through the door, with Lombard and Quaid behind him. He stood for a moment, looking at the two rangers.

'I've got some news for you two,' he said. 'You'll be going riding before daybreak tomorrow. There's a Comanche I know pretty well, name of Red Eagle. I sell him a few guns now and then. I rode out to see him yesterday. He and his band are camping in a ravine twelve miles west of here, and they'll be moving on tomorrow.

'But before they leave,' he went on, 'we're going to hand you two over to him, and they're going to kill you, in the Comanche way, so that when your bodies are found, it'll be clear who did it. He didn't need any persuading to do the job, because he ain't got no love for rangers, but all the same, I promised him that big white horse, and the pinto, and some more guns the next time I see him.'

He smiled sardonically.

'Hope you both rest easy tonight,' he said, and left, followed by the other two.

When they had gone, the two rangers continued working at the window, and well before the time was due for the evening meal to appear, they had completed the chiselling which would enable sufficient bars to be pulled out to allow them to climb out through the aperture. They sat on their bunks, and waited for the meal to appear. When they had eaten it, and the tray had been removed, Jack stepped onto the bunk, and levered one bar slightly forward with the chisel, so that it was possible to get a good grip on the bottom of it. It was now quite dark outside. He stepped down.

'You've got a stronger grip than I have,

Joseph,' he said. 'See what you can do with those bars that have to come out.'

Joseph climbed on the bunk, and grasping the bottom end of one bar after another, he exerted all his strength, and pulled them free, handing each one to Jack as he removed it. Then, followed by Jack, he climbed through the window, dropped to the ground, and ran to the derelict building. Jack had the hammer and chisel with him. Joseph had the knife. As they ran round the building, they heard a voice inside.

'Senores,' it said. 'This is Ramon. I have been waiting for you.'

It was unmistakably Ramon's voice. They went inside.

'Senores,' said Ramon. 'In the morning, Lombard and the others will be looking for you. You must leave town for a while. Follow me.'

He led the way along the backs of the houses, past Consuela's house, almost to the edge of town, and stopped outside a house where two mules were tethered. He led the way into the house, where a small lamp, turned low, was burning.

'This is my house,' he said. 'Take the mules. I have borrowed them for you. And ride that way.' He pointed to the east.

'There are many places where you can hide, not far from town. The mules are carrying enough food and water for a few days.'

'I think these are yours, Ramon,' said Jack, handing over the hammer and chisel.

'Yes,' said Ramon. 'I thank you for bringing them back to me. This is my best and sharpest chisel. It was Pepe, the son of my cousin, who stood on my shoulders, and dropped them into your cell. When you did not return to my sister's house, and I saw that the men who came for Juanita were free, a friend of mine watched the jail from the old building, and he saw you at the cell window. Please keep the knife, until you have no need of it.'

'I think, Ramon,' said Jack, 'that yesterday you were very busy in your blacksmith shop.'

'Very busy, senor,' said Ramon. 'All day I have worked at my anvil.'

'We thank you, Ramon,' said Jack.

He felt round the inside of the back of his vest, and from a small concealed pocket, he brought out a number of one hundred dollar bills.

'Ramon,' he said. 'We will need more than the knife to get the better of Lombard and the others. We must have guns and ammunition. Can you buy these things for us?'

'I will do this,' said Ramon, 'but I must buy them in such a way that the sheriff does not hear of it. I will get my cousin to bring them to you tomorrow afternoon, about four o'clock. He will bring them to the small ravine, about six miles to the east of here, with a single tree standing in the entrance. I will not bring them myself, because Lombard may suspect something if I am missing from my work.'

Jack thanked the Mexican, and handed some money over. Then he and Joseph mounted the mules, and headed east. They spent the rest of the night in the small ravine that Ramon had mentioned, and stayed there until the following afternoon, keeping a lookout for approaching riders. Just before four, they saw a solitary rider approaching from the west. They stayed just inside the ravine until the rider drew close, and they could see that he was a Mexican. Then they walked out to meet him.

'Buenas tardes,' said the rider. 'I am from Ramon. I bring the things you have asked for.'

He handed a sack over to Jack, who looked inside it. It contained two Colt .45 Peacemakers, with ammunition. Both guns appeared to be in good condition. He handed one to Joseph. They each loaded their gun, and holstered it, grateful that their gunbelts had not been removed by their captors.

Jack thanked the Mexican.

'You are welcome, senores,' he said, 'I have heard of how you have helped Juanita, the daughter of my cousin. Ramon has asked me to tell you that the sheriff, and the other men who kept you in jail have searched for you in the houses of all the Mexicans in Jurado. But of course, you were not found. Ramon asks you to come to his house after dark this evening.'

'Tell Ramon we'll be there,' said Jack, and the Mexican departed.

The rangers had a meal, then headed for Jurado. Darkness fell when they were half-way there. They approached Ramon's house from the back. There were three horses standing at the side of the house, and a light was on inside. There was the sound of shouting coming from the interior of the house, and then a sudden cry of pain. The rangers dismounted, and ran quickly round to the door, which was ajar. Jack pushed it open, and entered, gun in hand. Joseph followed close behind Jack, then stood beside him.

Inside the room, Ramon was crouching in

a corner, while Sully was striking him about the head with the lash of a heavy quirt. The Mexican's face was criss-crossed with weals, some of which were bleeding copiously. Standing watching the brutal beating, with their backs to the rangers, were Platt and Scriven, each holding a gun loosely by his side, muzzle pointing towards the floor.

As Sully raised his arm, ready to direct a further vicious lash at Ramon's face, Joseph threw the knife which Ramon had loaned them, and it penetrated deep into Sully's back, below the right shoulder. Sully screamed, and the quirt dropped from his hand. Platt and Scriven turned, and started to raise their guns. But before either had managed to fire his weapon, Jack shot Scriven, and Joseph shot Platt. Both men fell to the floor.

Joseph walked over, and disarmed Sully, who was sitting on the floor, groaning, with the knife still protruding from his back.

Jack walked up to Platt and Scriven, and bent over them, in turn. They were both dead. Then he walked up to Ramon, and helped him to a chair. He looked at the wounds on the Mexican's head and neck. Several were bleeding badly, but so far as Jack could tell, the eyes had not been damaged.

'We will take you to your sister, Ramon,' he said. 'Then we will go to find Lombard and the others. Why was this man Sully beating you?'

'They wished to find out where you and your friend were hiding, senor,' replied Ramon. 'They did not believe me when I said I did not know.'

Jack turned towards Joseph, who was standing over Sully.

'Bind and gag him, Joseph,' he said. 'Then we can go for the others. Will he be all right here for a spell?'

'He will live,' replied Joseph, 'but it is better that we leave the knife in his back until a doctor sees him.'

They left Sully lying on his side on the floor. Then they helped Ramon over to his sister's house. Jack knocked on the door, and Consuela opened it, Juanita by her side.

'Madre de Dios!' she called out, as she caught sight of her brother's cut and bleeding face. She ushered him to a chair at the table.

'Warm water, Juanita,' she called. 'Quickly.' She got a piece of cloth, and started to wipe the blood from Ramon's face.

'Senora,' said Jack. 'We must go now, to find the sheriff and the others.'

'Senor,' said Ramon, holding Consuela's hand away from his face for a moment, while he spoke. 'I think the man Farren and the sheriff will be waiting somewhere, for Sully to come and tell them where you are hiding. Maybe they will be in the Sheriff's Office, maybe in the saloon next to it. Be careful, both of you.'

The rangers left, and walked along to the Sheriff's Office. There was no light inside. They continued on towards the saloon, and stopped short of it.

'You go in from the back, Joseph,' said Jack. 'I'll give you a couple of minutes before I go in.'

Joseph nodded, and headed for the rear of the building. When the two minutes had elapsed, Jack walked up to the swing doors of the saloon, pushed them open, and walked inside. Immediately, he saw Lombard, sitting with Farren and Quaid, at a table near the far end of the saloon. He started walking towards them, and had reached a point only a few yards away, when Lombard glanced in his direction, and saw him.

Seeing the look on Lombard's face, his two companions followed his gaze, and also saw Jack. All three rose slowly to their feet. A hush gradually fell on the saloon, and customers hastily moved out of the possible lines of fire. Keeping his eye firmly on the three in front of him, Jack spoke to the other occupants of the saloon.

'In case you don't know it,' he said. 'I'm a Texas Ranger. I'm here to arrest Sheriff Lombard, and the two men with him. Those two are robbers, and the sheriff is in cahoots with them. I aim to put them in the jail, and keep them there till they go for trial.'

As the three men stared at Jack, nerving themselves to go for their guns, Joseph, walking from behind the bar, held a gun on them from behind.

'Don't do it,' he said, and they froze momentarily. Joseph pulled Quaid's gun from its holster, then jammed the muzzle of his Colt against Farren's neck. Desperately, Lombard, throwing caution aside, went for his gun. He made a fast draw, but the observers in the saloon who were closely watching Jack, witnessed a draw that was so smooth, speedy and precise that Jack's bullet penetrated Lombard's heart before the sheriff had fired.

Farren, Sully and Quaid were held in jail until Sully's knife wound was almost healed. Then the three of them were taken to El Paso for trial. Farren received a long prison sentence. Sully and Quaid, on account of their part in the lynching, were hanged.

The two rangers returned to Amarillo, where Jack resigned from the Rangers, and parted from Joseph.

Two days after this, Todd Burley and his daughter Mary were sitting in the Lazy B ranch-house, relaxing after the midday meal. Burley was dozing, and Mary was sitting in a chair near the window, looking towards the south. Suddenly she jumped up, and ran outside. The noise of the door slamming behind her woke the rancher. Moments later, he caught sight of his daughter through the window, riding off, bareback, at speed.

'What the...!' he shouted to himself. Quickly, he got up, and ran out of the house. He looked after Mary. She was heading south, at the fastest pace she could muster. Then, looking beyond her, Burley suddenly understood, and smiled. A rider on a big white horse, one arm upraised in greeting, was racing towards his daughter.

The publishers hope that this book has given you enjoyable reading. Large Print Books are especially designed to be as easy to see and hold as possible. If you wish a complete list of our books please ask at your local library or write directly to:

**Dales Large Print Books**
Magna House, Long Preston,
Skipton, North Yorkshire.
BD23 4ND

This Large Print Book, for people
who cannot read normal print,
is published under the auspices of

**THE ULVERSCROFT FOUNDATION**

... we hope you have enjoyed this book.
Please think for a moment about those
who have worse eyesight than you ...
and are unable to even read or enjoy
Large Print without great difficulty.

You can help them by sending a
donation, large or small, to:

**The Ulverscroft Foundation,
1, The Green, Bradgate Road,
Anstey, Leicestershire, LE7 7FU,
England.**
or request a copy of our brochure for
more details.

The Foundation will use all donations
to assist those people who are visually
impaired and need special attention
with medical research, diagnosis
and treatment.

Thank you very much for your help.